Coyote Summer

Catherine Maven

Otter-Girl Press

Burlington, Ontario, Canada

https://sleepingcat.wixsite.com/ottergirlpress

DEDICATION

This book is dedicated to my amazing partner, George, and my three wonderful sons – Russ, Tim, and Dean – who have always been a source of joy, pride, and deliciously-absurd laughter; to my most excellent step-kids Adriana & James, who have added new richness to my life; to my awesome in-law kids, Sheruni, Timothy, Clement & Marie, with my deepest gratitude for making my kids happy; and to my friends (you know who you are) for helping to keep me sane when the world seems to be going extra-crazy.

I love you all!

CONTENTS

Chapter One:

The young coyote had gotten up before dawn to taunt cows, while they weren't alert enough to be dangerous. That part was fun. The fun ended when she couldn't find anything to eat afterward, and by the time she'd run the six miles back home to her den, she was too tired to even look for food. So when she was awakened what seemed like only a couple of hours later, she was irritable enough to want to bite the first thing she saw when she climbed out of her den.

Things, actually. The source of the noise that had dragged her from a lousy, hungry sleep turned out to be a pair of crows. They were perched on a fallen log, singing a discordant duet, heads bobbing in time as they cawed.

They shut up when they saw her approaching, her tail tucked under and her ears back. Their iridescent blue-black heads glinted in the light as they tilted their heads in unison to look at her. Shiny dark brown eyes gazed unblinkingly into her angry golden ones. Just as the coyote got close enough to spring at them, they calmly hopped down from the branch to land obligingly at her feet. She opened her jaws to snap off the nearest head, but hesitated as she panted to taste their scent. Finally, she stepped back and sat down with a disgusted sigh. It would have been polite to look away, but she refused, meeting the eyes of both birds in a challenging way. 'You started this,' the coyote thought. 'I'm just finishing it.'

Sure enough, the birds began to waver before her eyes, stretching upward, changing shape, feathers melting smooth. Despite the overhanging trees, shafts of sunlight stabbed the coyote's eyes as she looked up at them, and she blinked in pain. It had been a long night, and it looked like it was going to be a long day.

Silhouetted against the sun, two dark shapes were coalescing where the two birds had been cawing noisily a moment before. As they solidified, she saw she'd been right.

It was the 'twins' – cousins they said, but looking enough alike to be twins – Teesha and Tosha.

"Codi?" the girl on the right began uncertainly.

"Girl, we like, gotta talk, so shift," said the other, Teesha – or was it Tosha? – her voice dismissing her cousin's doubts.

Squinting against the bright light, the coyote couldn't help staring up at them. As annoying as the two girls acted, she was pained to admit they were even more annoyingly cute. Sleek, athletic bodies with flawless ebony skin. Hair so black it looked blue in the sunlight. Laughing brown eyes that seemed wise beyond their years. Dressed, as always, in identical Nike gear that somehow managed not to look ridiculous with their high platform sandals. After a moment, ignoring the pleading in their eyes, she turned and went back deep into her den.

The girls trotted unsteadily across the pine-needle-strewn ground to crouch at the almost invisible opening in the roots of the gigantic tree.

"Ah, Code, girl, we're sorry to bug you."

"Yeah, we wouldn't do it, really really really, if it wasn't really really important, ya know?"

…

"Is she still in there? Is there another exit?"

"Like I would know. I look like a Canis latrans geek to you?"

"Well, actually, now that you mention it –"

"Don't see you reaching in to get her out."

"Don't see you –"

"Eeeek!" The girls screeched in unison as the coyote leapt out of the den straight at them. They fell backward into the dirt, and the coyote trotted triumphantly off into the bush.

"Codiii –" Teesha called after her.

"Aw, dang!" Tosha sighed. "That girl always was hard to pin down."

Codi knew the girls vaguely from high school, but never had been able to tell them apart. It hardly mattered because they were always together anyway. Still, their valley-girl-slash-fake-ghetto-slang vocabulary and fashion fanaticism bugged her on principle.

A moment later, barefoot but dressed as usual in jeans and a t-shirt – today's slogan reading, "Your karma just ran over my dogma" – Codi walked back toward them slowly, looking around and drinking in the colors invisible to coyote eyes. The slanting light coming through the trees told her that it was late in the day. She must have slept longer that she'd thought. Still, she couldn't help sighing. What made the girls think they had the right to disturb the peace and privacy she'd come out here to ensure?

"Just tell me what you want, Teesha," she snarled as she leaned with practiced nonchalance against the tall pine that shaded the entrance to her den. When the girl on the left answered, she congratulated herself on solving the identity problem without admitting anything. She made a note that Teesha was the one wearing the green beads in her tightly-braided hair. Green, Teesha, blue, Tosha, she repeated silently as she listened to the crow girl's answer.

"Sorry to, like, wake you up, miss grumpy-pants. Ya can't sleep all summer, ya know."

Before responding, Codi stared at them in silence for a minute. "I don't think there was once all year I got as much sleep as I needed. Up all day going to school and half the night hunting with my parents. What's it to you?"

"Chill out, sista," said Teesha. "Where's your famous sense of humor?"

"Yeah, you've had, like, weeks to grab zees, girl," said Tosha. "Ya must be rested by now."

Sometimes Codi didn't think she would ever get enough sleep, but she didn't feel up to an argument because she knew the girls would actually enjoy it and she wouldn't. "So, I'm up. What do you want?"

The girls looked at each other as if communing telepathically, and then Teesha spoke. "It's this rabbit girl named Pook."

"Yeah, she's like, hooked up with a gang in the city," said Tosha.

"Bad news, Code. Drugs, violence, the total works."

"So?" Codi said. "That would be my business because? ... Rabbits are prey as far as I'm concerned. And what kind of a name is Pook, anyway?"

"Pook's real name is Renata. Her parents are like, Latvian, or somethin'. She's only fourteen or fifteen. C'mon, girl, ya gotta help us rescue her," said Teesha.

"Did she ask for my help?"

The girls looked at each other. "No, she –"

"Did she ask for your help?"

"It's not like that. We think she's in danger."

"Who do you think you are? Batman and Robin? No, wait – make that Batgirl and Cat Woman?" Codi thought she might enjoy this after all.

"Ya got us all wrong, Codester," said Teesha.

"Yeah," insisted Tosha. "You the oldest Shifter here who is Testing this summer. Ya gotta, like, take responsibility, ya know."

"Just because our parents left us alone doesn't make me anybody's babysitter," Codi argued, looking at her shadow, which showed that her short, spiky dirty-blond hair was currently suffering from major bed-head.

It made her grumpier than ever. Nevertheless, she could feel a tug in her guts, and she didn't like the feeling. Bad enough that she'd had to wait until the summer after she graduated from high school to do the Test.

When she had pushed hard for the right to prove she was old enough to be on her own, though, it had never occurred to her she might end up as the mom to the group of a dozen or so teenage Shifters who were also Testing for independence.

Their parents, like hers, had taken the younger Shifters and gone to some unknown and unreachable place for the summer, giving their older offspring the chance to prove they were ready to take responsibility for their own lives.

"Shifters like, look out for their own," said Tosha.

"Yeah, just 'cause you don't take nothin' seriously don't mean we don't care," added Teesha.

"Why's she Testing if she's only fourteen?" Codi crossed her arms over her almost non-existent breasts. "And you don't care you're going to make her fail her Test?"

"Technically, since we like, only Tested last year, we're not full 'adults'. So not only does our concern not make Pook fail, it's our, like, duty to look out for the Testing kids," said Tosha primly. "Which you would know if you hung out with other Shifters long enough to learn anything about your people." The pretty crow girl tossed her head angrily, causing her beaded braids to fly about her head like Medusa's snakes.

Codi opened her mouth to ask whether she was about to be turned to stone, but Teesha interrupted, perhaps mistaking her smirk for encouragement.

"Yeah, like, it's your duty as the oldest Tester in the area to look out for the younger ones. We're not calling the cops. We don't want to make Pook fail. We're just worried about her." She looked at Codi pleadingly.

Codi had gone to human schools since she was six, but spent her free time alone or in the company of coyotes like herself, and that had always suited her just fine. "Strength in solitude," was her father's favorite saying, part of what he called The Coyote Way, and Codi agreed. Mostly.

"What you mean is you crows are gossips and busybodies," she said, then felt bad when she saw the look of pain on Teesha's face. After a moment, though, she steeled herself. Whenever possible, she preferred to live out in the forest where few Shifters seemed to go. She was enjoying her freedom even more this summer while her parents were away, and didn't want these girls dragging her along while they stuck their noses into someone else's business.

This 'Pook' girl, whoever she was, was no concern of hers. But she knew before they said another word that the girls weren't going to leave it alone.

"Don't play, like, so hard to get, Code," said Teesha.

"We just wancha to go have a chat with her is all," said Tosha.

"Why don't you two go have a chat with her yourselves?"

"We've tried and tried," whined Tosha. "Pecked at the skylights like crazy, but she, like, just didn't see us."

"Oh, yeah? So how exactly am I supposed to be able to chat with her any better than you?" Codi challenged, meeting their stares levelly. "Just walk into some gang headquarters and politely ask to take away one of their girls? That ought to make me just popular enough to get knifed."

"Go in coyote form," suggested Teesha so quickly that they

had to have discussed it before coming. "You're the Trickster, aren'cha?"

"Yeah, bark like a dog, Lassie," laughed Tosha. "Like they're gonna know the difference. All we wancha to do is remind the girl to shift from time to time. She forgets to shift much longer, she's gonna be stuck being human. Period. Oh, and get her outa there if it looks like she's in danger, ya know?" Tosha tipped her head sideways in an annoyingly birdlike movement.

"Well," Codi said, hating herself for falling for such obvious manipulation. In their animal forms, the girls would also have been nothing but prey to her – if she hadn't been able, like all Shifters, to recognize another of her kind. But in human form, she found emotions harder to ignore. Like sympathy. Like now.

"Girl, you know it's the right thing to do," said Teesha, sensing victory. She went for the kill. "Besides," she said with a warm smile that lessened her obvious manipulation, "if you succeed, you'll be adding to your rep as the Trickster. How many coyote girls your age have confronted a gang on their own turf?"

"Come on, Code, it'll only take a few hours of your precious time," Tosha finished.

Both girls were smiling at her, brown eyes pleading, white teeth gleaming against dark skin. Codi suddenly realized how much the two girls resembled the famous tennis sisters, Venus and Serena, with infectiously warm smiles. Except the crow girls were about half the Williams sisters' size, she corrected herself. Codi was on the small side herself, and Teesha and Tosha were only a bit taller.

Codi didn't mind being short, though she knew humans often valued other people in proportion to their height, and at five-four, she didn't garner much of that kind of respect.

In her mind, her height, along with her skinny, boyish build, simply aided her in being as invisible in a group of people as her coyote self was so adept at being in the forest.

In fact, the only unusual things about her were her eyes, which were more gold than brown, particularly in strong sunlight. At school, she usually kept her eyes half closed to hide their uniqueness, giving her a sleepy look that hid her natural alertness and curiosity – making it that much easier to get away with pranks, her favorite pastime. She smiled as she remembered several especially inventive ones.

Hands together as if in prayer, the two girls were, for the moment, uncharacteristically silent as they waited for her answer.

"Okay, fine, I'll come check on her," Codi said finally, deciding it might be cool to treat the invasion of some gang headquarters as another prank. "But don't get too excited," she quickly added as the girls began to bounce up and down with glee, "because if this Pook chick doesn't want to leave, I can't, and I won't, make her. Understood?"

"Sure, Code, don't get yourself in a twist," said Teesha.

"So, like, are you gonna come now, or what?" asked Tosha.

Really, they sounded like two halves of the same self, Codi couldn't help thinking. Then something occurred to her. "How did you two know where my den was? It's supposed to be a secret."

"We have our sources," said Teesha, smiling mysteriously.

"We, like, know what we need to know when we need to know it," added Tosha smugly.

"Forget I asked," Codi said sarcastically. Still, there was no point in getting mad at them. No harm had been done, so far at least. Her natural good humor seemed to be returning. "So, are you guys going to fly back to the city, or did you bring your car?" she joked.

"Car," they said together, to her surprise. Oh, right. Rich girls.

"It's parked in the parking lot?" said Teesha as if Codi were mentally slow.

"You, like, know the one, about a mile thataway?" said Tosha, pointing unnecessarily. "You can change to coyote form here, or when we get to the city. Up to you. Either way, we gotta fly all the way back to the darn car. Why can't you, like, live in the city like civilized people?"

Codi ignored the jibe, considering for a moment before replying. "I guess I'll shift until we get to the parking lot, then go as I am … What day is it?"

The girls looked at each other and rolled their eyes. "Wednesday. Code, maybe you've been, like, spending too much time as a coyote. Ya gotta keep up with the human world, too, ya know," said Teesha.

"Fine. When we're done with your rabbit friend, I'll check on my place in town."

"Sounds like a plan, Stan," said Tosha.

"Yep, let's get in gear," said Teesha. "I'm, like, overdue for an ice cream while we're here trying to make you do what …" Seeing the look in Codi's eyes was enough to stop that particular train of thought in its tracks.

How the girls could eat the amount of sweets they were reputed to consume and still keep their slim bodies was a mystery, but not one Codi felt like investigating.

Instead, she shifted to coyote and trotted through the forest to the parking lot. She was panting from the heat she worked up over even that short distance. She had to admit she was grateful not to have to run the five or so miles into the city from her state park home in the August heat.

The girls were leaning against their car when she emerged from the woods in human form. "The shortest distance between two points is, like, to fly," smirked Tosha. "What took ya so long?"

"Hop in," said Teesha, holding the car door open. "Let's get goin'."

As Codi looked at their car, a silver Beamer, she let out a long, slow whistle. "Nice ride."

"It's only an '05," said Tosha defensively.

"Yeah, it's like, Mom's old car," added Teesha.

Without saying a word, Codi went straight past them to a maintenance shed at the end of the lot. She twirled the combination on the lock and a moment later pushed out her own sweet ride. "Thanks for the offer," she said, "but I'll just follow you."

"Oooh, a Kow!" exclaimed Teesha. "Cool!"

"Ancient is more like it," said Tosha, sounding like she was working hard not to be impressed. "How do ya keep that thing goin'? Crazy glue? Duck tape? Luck?"

"Hey, how come they, like, letcha keep your bike in there?" said Teesha.

"Told the groundskeeper I don't want my parents to know about it," said Codi, pulling on her helmet and straddling the motorbike. "Flashing a bit of belly when I asked didn't hurt either," she added with an evil grin. "You want to go, let's go."

Riding the motorbike along the silver ribbon that the highway became this late in the day was pure pleasure for Codi. But when the Beemer pulled off the road into a box mall on the edge of town, Codi almost turned the bike around and went back to the forest.

Her curiosity got the better of her common sense, though, so she followed the silver car around the parking lot until the car stopped in front of an ice cream parlor. Before she could even park the bike and take off her helmet to yell at the twins, Teesha had hopped out of the car and gone into the restaurant, so she was left to confront Tosha … At least, she thought it was Tosha. She couldn't remember which one had the green beads. That just made her madder.

"What's going on?" she snarled at the girl leaning casually against her car.

"Tosh went to grab you some food. You look hungry," said Teesha. Right. Green Teesha, blue Tosha. Whatever!

The fact that it was completely true somehow made Codi even madder. "What, now you're my Moms? I thought this Pook thing was an emergency!"

"Chill, Codester. We jus' tryin' to keep you happy. You gonna tell me that, like, you're not just a little bit hungry? Pook isn't in active danger – that we know of. We just want to keep it that way."

Just then, Tosha returned holding a paper bag in one hand and 3 cones in a tray in the other. "You want the ice cream first, or the burger and fries?"

Codi struggled to stay angry – hangry, actually. She could smell the food from here. "Listen, ladies, I appreciate your effort, but …"

Tosha strode over and shoved a cone into her hand. "You better start with the cone. It's melting. Reverse lunch!"

Codi wanted to drop the cone, climb on her bike, and go home. The trouble was, on top of being hungry to start with, she had to admit she had a bit of a sweet tooth, particularly in her human form.

Coyotes didn't usually have access to sweets, except for the juicy ripe berries she enjoyed whenever she could, and the desserts occasionally left behind by picnickers.

"Thanks," she said, licking around the cone to rescue the ice cream that was already dribbling down the sides.

Tosha put the food bag on the trunk of the car, and smiled as she licked her own cone. "Yum! Blueberry shortcake! My favorite!"

"Sorry, I don't have any money on me. I'll pay you back after I get back to my place in the city," she said after she had crunched through the last of the cone – way ahead of the girls, who were, typically, eating theirs in dainty bites.

"Forget it," said Tosha. "It's our way of thanking you for helping Pook out."

Codi was embarrassed. Now she felt as though they thought they had to buy her to get her to help! She tried to tell herself there was really nothing wrong with the girls buying her a bit of food, but still, she had refused the money her parents had tried to give her at the beginning of the summer, insisting that she could provide for herself in the human world as well as in the animal one.

Which reminded her how she'd failed her hunt that morning. So it felt like doubly cheating to eat something she didn't pay for, and hadn't earned herself. She shook off the guilty feeling, reminding herself a couple of bucks wasn't exactly going to break them. Besides, she was starved, so when Tosha handed her the bag of food and gestured toward a picnic table, she slouched over and sat down, opening the bag and leaning in to inhale the delicious aromas.

While they were eating, Codi asked the girls how they had found out about Pook.

"We like to keep tabs on our people, Code," said Teesha.

"Yeah, and we bet nobody ever thinks we're like, just plain nosy," said Tosha. Both girls laughed good-naturedly. It was hard to stay mad at them for very long, because their happy, friendly personalities thawed Codi's anger. She wasn't sure if their perkiness was genuine or fake, but she figured since she wasn't ever going to know, she might as well accept them the way they were.

"So when did you discover Pook was hanging out with this gang?"

"Coupla weeks ago, I guess," said Teesha.

"Yeah, we didn't worry at first, ya know, because it's, like, her life and all, but we don't think she's shifted once in all that time," said Tosha, her pretty face creasing into a frown.

"We're worried she's forgotten who she is," said Teesha, her smile also suddenly gone.

All three were silent for a few minutes, finishing their food. If Shifters spent too long in either form, animal or human, they could end up forgetting their other self.

Which in itself wasn't a disaster, except that Shifters were, if not exactly immortal, at least extremely long-lived, and spending too much time with humans meant sooner or later somebody was going to notice something was odd.

Shifters had lived invisibly among humans for thousands of years. The last group who had known Shifters for what they were were Native North Americans, who had accepted them as 'brothers and sisters', and whose legends were all that remained of the friendship that had ended with the arrival of the Europeans, who rejected all indigenous beliefs and legends, including those about half-animal, half-human creatures.

Since then, Shifters had lived in secrecy and fear. No one wanted to be dissected or exterminated. Occasionally a Shifter would choose a human partner and marry, but if necessary, other Shifters always stepped in to hustle them away in time to ensure their shared secret remained safe.

What the rabbit was doing, Codi thought, was none of her business. Pook had been left by her parents to fend for herself for the summer.

Rabbits mature young, but are social creatures, preferring to live in groups, like most prey animals. It made sense she had found a group to join.

Codi knew that gangs could be bad news, but from her point of view, they were somebody else's bad news. Not her circus, not her monkeys. Really, the only unfortunate thing would be if Pook got hurt or accidentally revealed her animal self while high on something.

Despite Codi's feeling that they were butting into something that was none of their business, when they were done eating, she followed the girls' car through increasingly rundown streets. They were entering the warehouse section of town when Tosha finally stopped the car and Codi pulled in behind her. Codi took one look around and decided no place could be farther from her beautiful home in the forest. Concrete sidewalks without so much as a weed growing up through them. Not a tree in sight. Tall, soot-smudged buildings that looked abandoned. This area had been ugly in its heyday, and it had been decades since then. There were broken windows everywhere, with cardboard taped over them or left open to the elements. The air smelled worse than death, and as an occasional carrion eater, Codi ought to know. The claustrophobia she always felt in the city closed in on her.

Pushing the feeling aside, she nodded her head toward the nearest building and whispered, "Is this where she is?" She wasn't sure why she was whispering, but she had no experience with what a TV show she'd seen had called 'covert ops', so she wasn't sure how to proceed.

"I don't think so," said Tosha loudly and sarcastically, making Codi blush. "It's about six blocks thataway. You like, don't wanna park inside the gang's territory."

"Yeah," said Teesha, "they're, like, worse than the parking police. Ya get a smashed windshield for parking in the wrong spot around here."

"Or worse. Strip your car to the, like, bare metal, ya give 'em a chance."

"How do you know where the territory starts?" Codi asked, feeling suddenly a lot younger than the two girls, when in fact they had graduated from her high school only a year earlier.

"There," said Teesha impatiently, pointing.

Codi looked where she'd pointed, and saw some graffiti on the side of a building. "Yeah, so what?"

"Says 'Strykers' if you read it backwards," explained Tosha.

She stared at the graphic for a minute, baffled. It looked like swirling nonsense to her, but she didn't want to admit it and look even stupider than she felt. So she just nodded, but from Tosha's smirk Codi suspected the other girl knew she didn't get it. "Why 'Strykers'?" she asked as a distraction.

"Sort of a pun on how this useta be a steel town, and like, how the unions useta run everything, back b'fore the corporations replaced all the workers with robots in the, like, new factories they built in China, ya know?" Tosha waited a beat and added, "That, and the fact they're pretty violent criminals, 'strike-ers'. Ya know, gang wars, knockin' over convenience stores and old ladies, the usual ganger hobbies."

Codi could see they were watching her to see how shocked she was, so she kept her face neutral. How did rich girls like these know so much about gangs? She decided she didn't really want to know. "Okay, what's the next step, oh wise city-gods?"

She was rewarded with frowns that showed her jibe had hit home, and then Teesha broke in, as if anxious to ease the tension. "See that alley over there? You go in, shift. Trot on down this street to a gray building with a huge black garage door, about eight blocks."

Tosha continued. " You can't miss it. Go in with your tail wagging, ya know, and those proles will, like, never know you not jus' a cute little doggie. Check out what the Pookster is doing, and if ya get her alone, see if ya can remind her to get away in animal form for a few minutes. Got it?"

"Okay …" Codi said without enthusiasm. "What if they shoot dogs?"

"Just shift into bareass human," laughed Tosha. "Your skinny white butt oughta freak 'em enough to give ya time to escape."

Teesha put her hands on her cousin's shoulders and was laughing with her, the beads in their braids rattling, while Codi worked hard to gather what remained of her dignity. "I don't see you girls putting yourselves on the line here."

"Okay, okay, you're right," said Teesha, controlling herself with an effort. "Tosh, calm down. Seriously, Code. I don't think these dudes would shoot a dog, but all we've done is look in through the skylights. We've like, been trying to get Pook to look up, but either she couldn't hear us or was too stoned to care. We didn't see any guns on 'em, though." She looked at her cousin, who nodded in confirmation.

Codi felt she'd procrastinated long enough. If she was going to do this thing, she had to just do it. "Okay, are you guys leaving, or are you going to watch from the skylights again?"

"Skylights, girl. We got your back."

"Great," she said, hoping she sounded like she meant it. "See you there in, say, five minutes?"

"Done and donner." The girls headed for another dark alley, and Codi went to shift into coyote form.

She slunk out of the shadows a minute later, hating the fact there was nowhere to hide. Her natural instincts were to lurk and blend into the background. At the moment, she also hated her coyote's sense of smell, for if she'd imagined the place stank before, she now wanted to retch. There was death here all right. She wasn't about to go looking for it, though, so she raised her tail up as high as she could, doglike, and trotted down the sidewalk as if she'd lived here all her life. She had gone to the trouble of rolling in some dirt in the alley, so she would look more like a stray, and she hoped her 'disguise' would work.

She quickly found the building with the black garage door the girls had mentioned. Sure enough, the same graffiti logo was painted above a window. She looked higher, and from the edge of the roof a black bird with a beautiful indigo bird flapped her wings at her. Imagining that the large truck-loading doors onto the street probably wouldn't be the one the gang used, Codi trotted around the back of the building and up the alley.

About half-way along she found a door propped open with a rock, releasing a steady draft of the heat tapped inside. No one was guarding the door, so she cautiously squeezed herself through the opening. She found herself in a long narrow hallway. Her sensitive ears picked up the sound of voices straight ahead, so she forced herself forward at a jaunty trot. Think of this as another prank, she repeated to herself over and over so she wouldn't think about the danger. Then she switched her mental voice to the false perkiness of an infomercial narrator: "It's not dangerous, it's fun!"

The hall opened into an echoing, cavernous warehouse space. Codi paused in the shadow of the doorway, scanning the layout. A living space had been created on the far side by placing dilapidated, pungently-aged sofas and chairs in a rough half-circle facing the doorway, with a few tables covered in empty pizza boxes and beer cans scattered in between.

There were about a half a dozen young people in the room, their exact ages and races hard to guess from this distance. The boys were all dressed in the pre-requisite dew-rags, baggy rapper pants and dirty t-shirts. There were three girls, and Codi cursed herself for not getting a description of the rabbit-girl. After watching for a moment, however, she realized that only one of them could possibly be Pook.

She was the hyperkinetic one, laughing and, well, hopping from boy to boy, touching, talking non-stop. Not five feet tall, she barely came up to the boys' shoulders.

Light brown hair, highlighted in what was probably a variety of fluorescent colors (Codi hated being color-blind when she was a coyote), low-slung jeans, and a crop top which revealed the baby fat still visible on her pale-skinned midriff, along with the prerequisite belly-button ring.

Whew! Codi felt like sitting down. Pook was definitely no more than fourteen. Damn! Why had her parents abandoned her to the Test at such a young age?

She reminded herself she wasn't supposed to care, once again lifted her tail as much as possible into dog position, and trotted into the room. As preoccupied – or stoned – as the group was, it took a full minute for anyone to notice her. She saw that she needn't have worried about getting shot – not only were there no guns visible, but all three girls quickly ran forward to embrace her.

Every wild instinct she had made her want to snarl at the apparent 'attack', but today Codi was a small golden-haired dog, so she sat down and endured the coos and cuddles.

All of the girls were just a little out of it – high, Codi figured. This complicated matters. How was she supposed to communicate with a stoned Shifter?

Before she was able to catch Pook's glassy-eyed attention, the boy gangers noticed they were no longer getting the girls' attention and came over, roughly pulling them away from the 'dog'. The girls weren't the passive victims Codi had imagined, however, for two of them immediately pulled themselves free and returned to caressing her.

"This yo' dawg?" a tall, dark-skinned boy asked Pook, his voice casual but his hand tightly gripping her upper arm.

Codi saw a frightened look flash across Pook's eyes for a moment, and wondered if the girl might be in danger after all.

But Pook recovered quickly, yanking her arm away from the boy. "Not mine," she said, her voice rabbit-soft, but with an edge of anger to it. She was rubbing her arm where he'd gripped her. "Jelly? She yours?" she asked another girl.

Before the other girl could answer, Codi felt someone grab her tail. As she turned, baring her fangs in anger, she saw that it was the boy Pook had broken free of, except now he had a long-bladed knife in his hand, looking like he was preparing to cut Codi's tail off.

"What you think, dawgs? Git me a dawg tail o' m'own?" the boy laughed, lifting Codi off her hind feet. Codi hadn't really been worried until then, because she knew she could probably bite the boy's hand before she had a chance to cut her, but with her hind feet up, it wasn't going to be so easy.

"'S'only tail you gonna git, ugly muther like you," said a Latino boy, and everyone roared with laughter while the dark-skinned boy looked madder and madder.

Now Codi felt real fear gripping her guts. The ganger was no doubt high, and maybe mad enough to actually cut off her tail. As a Shifter, she knew she could make another one, but Shifters possessed no immunity to pain.

Or bullets. "You want, I shoot her for ya, make it easier to git that tail," said a boy who looked like a Latino-Asian cross, pulling a handgun out of a deep pocket in his jeans.

"Shoot! Shoot! Shoot!" chanted the boys who had remained seated. They were leaning forward, excitement lighting up their glassy eyes. Codi closed her eyes.

Then she felt soft warm arms wrap around her, and opened her eyes to see Pook kneeling between her and the gun. She wanted to lick her face, but thought she might not appreciate that kind of gratitude. "Jelly, I said, is this your dog?" Pook asked the girl beside her.

"Yeah," said the girl, catching on, her eyes defiant as she looked up at the boys. "She looks just like my dog ... Goldie." She knelt down and scratched Codi behind the ears. "'Zat you, Goldie?" Codi reluctantly licked the girl's face, while deciding 'Jelly' was at most a year older than Pook. She was too skinny – drug-skinny. She had a very pale face under greasy black hair, and was wearing black lipstick and nail polish, black tank top and tights, and black army boots that laced up to her knees. Her arms were tattooed with snakes, which usually gave Codi the creeps, but she wasn't about to criticize one of her rescuers.

"Got big ears, don't she?" Jelly added, scratching them again.

This made one of the boys laugh, a little too loudly. "All the better to hear you with, my dear," he growled, and the rest of the room cracked up.

"Zat it, dawg? You really a wolf come here to eat these little girls up?" said the Latino boy. The other ganger let go of her tail, his good humor having apparently returned, and Codi's hind legs thumped back onto the floor. She looked around. The gun was nowhere in sight. She was glad the gangers would never guess how close they were to the truth – Codi was, in fact, cousin to the wolf.

"She's probably come lookin' for handouts," said the third girl, who was, if anything, younger than Pook, her purple hair, dozen earrings, and liberal makeup not quite enough to hide the childish roundness of her face. Codi didn't like it, even though the boys didn't look much older than the girls. In fact, no one in the room looked more than seventeen.

Still, it made sense. Younger, and they might have parents looking for them. Older, and they were either professional criminals, in jail, or gone straight. She wondered just exactly what she was supposed to do here.

Eat a donut for starters, apparently. A fat Hispanic kid had brought over a donut, and Codi played her part, bouncing on her feet and wishing she was able to wag her tail.

"See?" said Pook. "She's just hungry."

The fat boy tossed Codi the donut, which she swallowed in two gulps, and looked up for more. She was determined to be as doglike as possible, which wasn't that hard because she actually loved donuts.

This seemed to be the wrong thing to do, however, for now the fat boy looked annoyed. "Go on, get outa here!" he said, aiming a kick at Codi's head, which Codi easily dodged.

"Hey!" Jelly said. "Leave her alone!"

"Get it outa here," repeated the fat kid in a menacing tone, and Codi decided this kid must be the leader, because all of the others were instantly on their feet.

When Pook began to walk back toward one of the couches, though, Codi followed her, hoping she wasn't about to get shot after all.

"Think she likes you," said the Latino-Asian boy. "Dawg knows prime meat when it sees it." This made everyone laugh, and the tension eased.

Jelly took the opportunity to say, "Pook, grab 'nother donut to lead it outside, throw it, 'n shut the door. Goldie will find her way home."

Pook looked doubtful until the fat boy okayed the suggestion with a nod of his head. Then she reached over, grabbed a donut out of a box, and began to back toward the doorway.

Codi followed obediently, and everyone clapped. She had the feeling they were all just a little bored.

Once they were alone in the dim hallway, Codi yipped at her, trying to get Pook to make eye contact, which should have been enough to make her aware of her Shifter self.

It didn't work, and Codi wasn't sure if Pook had been human too long or whether she was too high to focus. As they neared the doorway, she saw her opportunity slipping away, so she sat down, refusing to get close enough for the other girl to throw the donut.

"Come on, dog, it's for your own good," coaxed Pook. "You don't wanna make those boys angry." She moved forward, waving the donut closer to Codi's nose. When she was only a couple of feet away, Codi allowed her face to begin shifting into human. Pook's eyes went wide, and she gasped in fear. Then recognition hit the rabbit girl, and her own nose was suddenly tiny and pink, looking comical in her human face.

A second later they had both returned to their previous states, but Codi was sure the message had been received. She stood up, licked her nose, and followed Pook as she headed for the door. The rabbit girl threw the donut far into the alley, and Codi ran out, but immediately turned back to look at Pook before she closed the door. It was only because of her sensitive coyote ears that she heard the girl whisper, "Thanks." The door closed, and Codi was alone in the alley.

She looked up. The two crows cawed once from the roof edge, and took off in the direction of their car. Gobbling the donut on the way by (why waste food?), Codi quickly trotted back toward the car, found an alley, shifted, and emerged just as the girls did.

She couldn't help noticing they were back in their standard uniform, black sports bras and spandex bike shorts, all of it skin-tight. She wondered how they could be so brazen. Her own nature demanded a little more subtlety.

When they met at the vehicles, Teesha said, "How'd it go?"

"Fine, I think. I got her alone for a second in the hallway, and we both partly shifted. I'm pretty sure she knows what she has to do."

"Good job, Code."

"Ace!" said Tosha. "And look at it this way. You like, got paid for your efforts – in donuts!"

Both girls were laughing, but Codi resisted the temptation to deny she had enjoyed them.

"So that's it," she said instead, keeping her face neutral. "Now, can we all go back to minding our own business?"

That sobered them up. "Don't know, Code," said Teesha. "D'ya think she's, like, using?"

"Yeah, maybe. Hard to tell. She was hyper as hell, but then, she's, like, a rabbit, isn't she?" If they noticed her sarcastic use of their valley-girl accent, they gave no sign.

"Well, we'd better keep an eye on her for another week or two. Like yours, her parents're due back in a few weeks, and I, like, wouldn't wanna hafta tell 'em she'd gotten hurt 'cause we weren't watchin' out for her."

Codi wanted to ask how babysitting a rabbit had become the responsibility of a pair of crows. Pook didn't appear to be in any real danger, and if what she'd seen was any indication, this wasn't the ugliest gang in the city.

Still, as much as she told herself that it was none of her business, that Pook was free to spend her summer surviving her own way, just as she was, she couldn't help worrying.

She hadn't liked the situation all that much, especially the way that ganger had grabbed Pook's arm. Still, she decided to say nothing more for the moment.

Tosha insisted on following her in their car to the basement apartment which was her human habitation. It was in another aging section of the city, but one that had been maintained with the kind of dignity some people manage in spite of poverty.

"Thanks again, Code," said Teesha through the car window as Codi pulled off her helmet. She reached out and pressed a scrap of paper into her hands. "Our cell numbers. In case, you know, anything ..."

"Yeah girl, you like, really came through," said Tosha, leaning across her cousin to smile at her. "You take care, okay?"

"I'll be fine. So will Pook. I think you should just let her be." And leave me out of it, she didn't add out loud. She watched them drive away, and then walked around back of the house toward her own entrance. The house was built on a hill, and so the basement apartment had a doorway leading out at ground level.

She retrieved her key from the top ledge of the window and was unlocking the door when she heard Mr. Gardiner.

"Hello, young lady," the old guy was saying, having magically appeared on the balcony over Codi's door as he did whenever Codi arrived.

Codi obediently backed out until she could see old guy. "Hi, Mr. Gardiner. How are you? How's Mrs. Gardiner? Better, I hope?"

"I'm as fit as a fiddle, and Marie is hardly limping any more. She's lucky she didn't break her hip. Shouldn't have been on a ladder at her age, you know."

This was almost word for word the conversation they'd had the previous Friday, the last time Codi had been here. She usually only showed up on Fridays, because she played with a band on Friday and Saturday nights. The Gardiners seemed to have accepted that their renter, as a musician, was a nomad, and had politely refrained from asking where she spent the rest of the week. She was grateful. She didn't like having to make up stories when there was no prank involved.

"I'm glad to hear Mrs. Gardiner is getting better. Remind her next time she gets out the ladder that I'll do the windows any time she wants."

"Yes, yes, well, you know how independent she is," said Mr. Gardiner. "You're here early this week?" Though they often told Codi they didn't like to pry into anyone's private life, she knew the old couple couldn't help wondering about her odd schedule.

"Yes, I've come down to practice with the band tonight," said Codi, realizing she could actually do that if she got changed and walked downtown.

One of the attractions of this place, besides the cheap rent, had been its proximity to the club where she played. The rest of the Latin dance band, 'Las Estrellas', had known from the beginning that their conga-drum player wasn't going to rehearse with them in any regular way.

Because Latin rhythms were so natural to Codi, she really didn't need to practice anyway. To her, they were all coyote heartbeats: mambo was the slow pounding of anticipation when she scented food, merengue was fast and simple like the chase, rumba catalana was the quick, driving beat of coming in for the kill, and salsa was the elation of catching her prey.

She brought her attention back to the moment. Mr. Gardiner had been talking, and she hadn't been listening. She really tried, but the old man's range of conversation wasn't great. Codi tried to be polite, but she found herself tuning him out as often as not.

"... back when we went dancing every Friday," Mr. Gardiner was saying.

"I wish I could have seen the two of you dancing together," Codi repeated, as she had the last six times the topic had come up. "Really, when her ankle heals, the two of you should come down to the club. We do some slow stuff, too, you know."

Mr. Gardiner smiled. "Latin dancing is for the young. Geezers like us have to stick to waltzes."

"I'll teach the band a waltz," Codi said, forcing a smile. "How's that?"

"You do that, and maybe we have a deal. Now, I'll leave you alone. You look a bit tired," said the old guy, turning away.

"Tell Mrs. Gardiner I said hi," Codi said loudly.

She had noticed that Mr. Gardiner seemed to hear just fine as long as you were face to face, but was somewhat deafer once his back was turned.

"I'll do that. Have a nice evening."

"You, too." Codi went back to her door, removed the key, and replaced it in its not-too-secret hiding spot. Despite the fact that she much preferred her forest den to any human habitation, she'd grown fond of this place.

The door to her human 'den' opened into a tiny kitchen, which must once have been a summer kitchen. There was no room for a table, so she'd set a couple of tall stools beside the counter to eat. To the left was her 'living room', which consisted of a single ancient leather lazy-boy chair, which she'd rescued from the curb shortly after moving in and spent most of her time in, a thrift-store floor lamp for reading, and the expensive stereo which was the only luxury she'd allowed herself, other than the motorcycle, which she justified as necessary transportation to and from the forest.

Behind the kitchen was a small bedroom containing only her narrow single bed, a closet where her few clothes were piled on shelves, and an even tinier bathroom, where her knees nearly touched the door when she was sitting on the john. 'Cozy,' she remembered Mrs. Gardiner calling the place. Cramped was more like it, but Codi was saving her money for school in the fall.

She glanced up at the clock on the kitchen wall, and calculated that she had enough time for a shower and even a short nap before rehearsal began at nine.

Chapter Two:

The band rehearsed at the club they played at. There was no cover during rehearsals, because they would stop and start songs whenever someone made a mistake or wanted to change something. Codi just drummed; she stayed out of the creative decisions of the band. Even though tonight was only a rehearsal, it was thrilling to perform. Codi was just leaving the stage after saying goodbye and knuckle-bumping her bandmates at the end of the last set. She was high with the excitement she always got from playing and from the appreciation of the crowd.

That is, until she saw Nadeem and his twin sister Rashda come in, ask the bouncer a question and then follow his pointed finger toward her. She knew Rashda only slightly, and, after her experience with the crow girls, she couldn't help being bugged by this invasion into her out-of-school life. Still, she owed Nadeem, who had volunteered to tutor her to help her pass algebra last semester. He was kind of a nerd, and therefore completely oblivious to his nerdishness. As if to prove the point, he grabbed Codi's forearm then slid down into a finger-gripping handshake that Codi was sure he'd seen in a movie and thought made him look cool. Wrong. Rashda's handshake was more normal.

"Codi, my friend, sorry I missed hearing you play," said Nadeem, as perfectly polite as always.

"Yes, Codi, we've never had the pleasure," complained Rashda. "Nadeem here thinks this place is too – 'sexy' was the word I think he used – for us." She smiled, revealing deep dimples in her warm cinnamon-brown face.

Codi ignored the small talk, just stared at Nadeem. "What's up?" She felt wired, and was still moving her feet to the beat of the music she could feel in her blood, though the room was now silent. Still, she could tell from the look on the boy's face that he had not come here to chat.

"We need to talk to you," said Nadeem, "There's a problem ... but maybe this isn't a good time?"

"Easy, bro'," said Codi, forcing her feet to stop. "I'm not drunk or anything. Playing gets me hyped. I'll settle down in a minute." She wished she had gone back to the forest instead of coming in for the rehearsal. Another problem with Shifters? What the heck was going on this summer?

She turned and led the two over to the bar. "Coffee still on?" she asked the barman, who was only a few years old than Codi. "Enrique, these are ... friends of mine from school, Nadeem and his sister Rashda." It felt weird to use the "f" word. Codi didn't think of herself as having any friends. It suited her to be a loner. Strength in Solitude.

"Sure thing, Codi," responded the short, handsome Latino. He turned to Nadeem and Rashda, extending a welcoming hand over the bar. "Nice to meet you. Didn't know Codi had any friends. Get anything for you? The bar's 'sposed to be closed, but for good friends of Codi, I can make an exception. Beer?" His smile could have lit the stage, thought Codi.

"No, thank-you," said Nadeem, but Rashda nodded her head. "Perhaps a glass of water, if it wouldn't be too much trouble?" Nadeem and Rashda's raccoon Shifter mother had married a human guy from

India, and it was a rare coincidence that both he and his littermate –
twin – Rashda were born Shifters. Human-Shifter marriages seldom led
to Shifter offspring. While they didn't share their father's charming
accent, they did share his extremely courteous manners.

The barman smiled again when he gave Codi her coffee and the
others their water with ice and a wedge of lime, and then returned to
cleaning up. Codi's heart couldn't help going 'thump!' whenever
Enrique spoke to her. She knew he wasn't really even aware of her
except as part of the band, and since he was human, not someone she
should even think about romantically, but she couldn't help it. His dark
eyes and kind smile, his ready laugh, and yes, his bulging biceps, made
the hair on Codi's neck prickle.

She forced herself to stop looking at him, and turned back to
the raccoon Shifters. The place wouldn't shut down for an hour or so,
and Codi figured it was better to talk here than risk waking up the
Gardiners. She led them over to a table in the corner. "Okay, what's
the matter?" she said as soon as they were seated.

"Have you heard anything about Shifter kids going missing?"
began Rashda.

Codi couldn't believe it. Twice in one day? The expression
"den mother" was starting to gain new meaning – and not in a good
way. They were looking at her, so she had to answer. "What? No I
haven't, but I've been living out in the forest. What happened?"

"It started about two weeks ago. I heard that a couple of cats
had gone missing, but I didn't think much of it at the time. Cats can be
pretty nomadic, even older kittens like these, and they don't take it very
well when you stick your nose in their business."

Nadeem was speaking quickly, and his nerdy voice grated on
Codi's sensitive ears. Still, she nodded in agreement, thinking of Teesha
and Tosha. "Okay, so I'm gathering it got worse?"

"Remember that red-head who was in eleventh grade last year?" said Nadeem.

"Yeah, the one you thought was pretty? Named Ariana or something lofty like that?"

Nadeem blushed, glancing over at his sister. "Um, yeah, that's her. She's also missing, and you know how timid cardinals are. She'd never gone farther from home than the high school or library until now. Rash and I think they've all been kidnapped."

"Hey, hey, hey, now. Lighten up! You're jumping to conclusions, Sherlock. Isn't Ariana Testing this summer?"

"Sort of. Her parents went off for the summer to visit some relatives, but left her with her older brother. That's who told me. I had a da – I was supposed to see Ariana yesterday" – here Nadeem glanced nervously over at his sister, who rolled her eyes – "but Ariana's brother said she didn't come home from the library yesterday afternoon. He's really worried about her. He thinks she's too young to have gone off on her own."

Codi thought about Pook, who had probably been in ninth grade last year, and who appeared to be Testing for independence already, but she didn't say anything. "So why are you freaking out?"

"Well, Rash is worried," said Nadeem defensively. "Me, too. It's the duty of all Shifters who are Testing to look after each other."

"She's his girlfriend," announced Rashda, glaring at her brother. "You honestly thought I didn't know?"

Codi was getting sick of this drama. It was none of her business! "So why come to me? What makes you so sure these kids have been kidnapped, rather than just taken off for a few days? It sounds like you're over-reacting."

"No one knows where they are, and they didn't leave any notes," said Rashda.

"No notes from kidnappers, either, then? Has anyone talked to the adult Shifters in the city?"

"Not yet. We don't want to make a bunch of kids fail their Tests just because we're kinda paranoid … Can you help us look for them?"

There goes my peaceful summer, Codi thought. Why was everyone suddenly bringing their problems to her? She repeated her question out loud. "Why me?"

"Well, you're the oldest Shifter who is Testing …" said Nadeem with an apologetic tone. "We thought you might want to help."

Codi had delayed the Test longer than other kids because her life had seemed fine to her just the way it was. Her parents were liberal with permission, and Codi had never had any reason to want to do something against their wishes. Being a Trickster didn't apply to parents. It had never occurred to her that delaying the Test was going to end up meaning that she was somehow responsible for all the younger Shifter kids!

After a moment, though, she suppressed her resentment. Not only did she owe Nadeem for his help in school, but this might be even more serious than Pook's situation. "Do you have any leads?"

"Just that the only kids missing in the city seem to be Shifters who are Testing. There's nothing in the newspapers," said Rashda.

"Really? That is a bit scary. If they were kidnapped, the only one who would recognize Shifter kids is another Shifter. Right?"

"I know," said Nadeem. "Must be a rogue… or a nut."

"Do you have any other clues? I'm surprised the gossip twins, T-squared (the school nickname for the crow girls) didn't mention anything about this. The whole group of city Shifters must be in an uproar."

"I heard Teesha and Tosha were hovering around some rabbit or other."

"Boy, you city kids keep better track of each other than we do out in the woods. I just heard about the rabbit, a girl named Pook believe it or not, a few hours ago when the twins came and dragged me out to check on her."

Nadeem wasn't about to be side-tracked. "I have also heard rumors of a new Shifter in town, 'sposed to be Spanish, but I don't know if there's any connection. People are always suspicious of strangers, but maybe he is the one taking the kids."

"A Shifter? Spanish? Seems a bit of a stretch to go from a few teenagers taking off for a few days to a stranger kidnapping them."

"I don't know much more than that. If Teesha and Tosha's family were here, they'd know for sure. I never thought I'd miss those nosy, noisy birds, but they'd come in handy right now." Nadeem glanced over at her sister, who nodded in agreement.

Codi got up and took their empty cups back to the bar. "Enrique, anybody new been hanging around in the last couple of weeks?" she asked the barman, thinking this was the only section of town that was Hispanic, and this was the only Latino bar in it.

"New guy? Just a minute, I'll check with my mom. We take turns in the kitchen and tending bar, and it was her turn for the bar this week." Carmen was Enrique's mom, and nearly as nosy as the crow girls.

He returned a minute later with a strange expression on his face. "Mom says there was a strange man in here a few days ago. She obviously didn't think much of him. Said he was ugly – and a bit scary, too."

"Could I talk to Carmen?"

Enrique sighed. "Sure. I'll just go clean up the kitchen for her."

"I can help after I ask her a few questions," Codi said, feeling guilty.

"Nah, don't worry about it, I'm just joking. I'll go get her."

Because of her sort-of crush on Enrique, Codi always felt nervous whenever she was speaking with Carmen, though Carmen had never been anything but friendly and supportive to her.

Which made her feel more nervous, like she was sneaking around, even though Enrique was apparently oblivious to Codi's admittedly feeble female charms.

Carmen looked tired tonight, but smiled warmly and came out from behind the bar to kiss Codi on both cheeks. "You were magnífico tonight, as usual, my Latin-hearted gringa. Now, what can I do for you?"

Codi led her to the table where Nadeem and Rashda were waiting. After quick introductions, they asked Carmen about the stranger.

"What did he look like?" said Nadeem.

"Na so tall, but theeck in hees body," said Carmen, her Spanish accent making her words sound more dramatic. "Fat, jes, but weeth muscles too, I could tell. Had a silver streak through hees hair. Look dangerous to me. Hees leettle dark eyes was loco. They move constantly, though he meet weeth no one tha' I could see. I deen like heem."

"I don't suppose you got his name?" Codi asked.

"Sorry. From hees accent when he order hees drink, though, I can tell he is Latino – from Sout Amereeca."

"Do you have any idea where he's staying?"

"Not weeth anyone I know – and I know every one who espeak espaneesh around here."

"He doesn't speak English?"

"Hard to tell, m'hija. No one person espeak henglish een here, usually not even jou, Codi ... Now, unless I get you sometheen, I better help Enrique een the keetchen or he'll be complaineen for a week."

"Thanks, amiga ... Oh, one more thing. I heard some teenagers have disappeared or run away over the last two weeks. I don't get the papers. You read about it?"

"Really? No, nada. That's amazeen. Keeds disappear and it don' make the sees o'clock news? I have to check heet out," Carmen said, frowning.

Codi remembered too late that all of the missing kids were Shifters, and perhaps their parents wouldn't want media attention. She tried to play it down. "Maybe the rumors I've heard aren't true. Don't worry about it. If it's real, I'm sure the police are on it." Carmen had four kids younger than Enrique, so the possibility of a serial kidnapper wasn't just a news story to her. "Maybe just keep the kids indoors for the time being, I guess."

"Nunca. They outside every meenute o' de day," Carmen said, getting to her feet. "We may had to buy a hex-box after all." She didn't look very worried. Carmen's children apparently never strayed far from their apartment above the bar, and seemed ridiculously well-behaved to Codi, whose own parents had been requested to meet with the teachers or principals of her schools on a regular basis ever since kindergarten. On top of that, Codi thought but couldn't say, Carmen's kids weren't Shifters like all of the other missing children.

Codi stood and took Carmen's hand to thank her again. After the woman went back to the kitchen, she turned back to where her companions sat staring at the tabletop as if it held the secrets of the universe. "Nadeem, Rashda, we should go. They're about to lock up. What do you want me to do?"

Nadeem and Rashda were looking over her head, so Codi turned around.

Enrique stood behind her with a worried look on his face. "Mom said there are kids missing." He pulled over a chair, turned it around and straddled it, his arms across the backrest. "What's going on?"

Now Codi really was in a bind. What could she say?

"It's just rumors," said Nadeem, coming to the rescue. "We're not even sure it's true." He turned to his sister for confirmation. "We just like to worry, right, sis?"

"That's true," said Rashda, peeking at Enrique from beneath her thick eyelashes and blushing.

Enrique looked from one of them to the other, as if assessing. Then he stood, and put his hand on Codi's shoulder. She looked up – not too far up, because he wasn't much taller than her – and he said, "Codi, if you or your friends need my help, please come and ask me. I guess it's none of my business, but I might be able to help. Okay?"

He looked at bit hurt, and Codi's stomach tightened. Then she shook it off. Cute or not, this was indeed none of his business. She wasn't about to expose fellow Shifters. So she just smiled a fake smile, and said, "Thanks, Enrique, there's no emergency here – at least not at the moment. But thanks, I'll remember your offer."

He looked even more hurt, and just nodded to Nadeem and Rashda before turning and heading back into the kitchen. Codi felt terrible. But aside from revealing her – their – secret, what could she do?

As the raccoon Shifters picked up their things, she said, "Just give me a sec," and headed back to the stage for her jacket with her keys in the pocket.

She returned a moment later. "Let's go."

Once they were outside, Codi felt better. Crush or no crush, she wasn't about to get Enrique involved in Shifter business. "So, what's the plan?"

"You're off tomorrow, aren't you? Maybe we can get together when you get up, and go looking." Nadeem forced a smile, but Codi could see how worried he was. She suspected Nadeem wouldn't agree with "strength in solitude" right now. Maybe there's something wrong with us coyotes that we don't worry much, Codi thought. She was concerned about the missing kids, but thought the "rogue Shifter" theory a bit of a stretch.

Kids ran away all the time, and Shifters who were Testing might very well think they had every right to take off for a few weeks while their parents were away. There was certainly no law that said they couldn't. She suspected her friends were over-reacting, just as Teesha and Tosha seemed to be doing. Why couldn't people let other people be? Or at least let her be?

Well, she didn't think she had a choice. Nadeem was the closest thing to a friend that she had. "Okay, sure," she said, her voice flatter than she intended. "Though I'm sure we'll find they've all gone off together, rafting down the river or something." She smiled what she hoped was a reassuring smile. Life was so much easier as a loner!

"Yeah, I hope you're right, Codi. Okay, then, see you tomorrow?" said Nadeem, getting up, heading for the door, and holding it open for Rashda and Codi.

"Yep. About noon, if not earlier, okay?"

"Whenever. We don't want to bother you," said Rashda, pulling her sweater around her, though Codi found the August night balmy.

"No bother," Codi lied, turning to head home. 'Night."

"Yah, see you tomorrow."

***

Their search the following day confirmed that two older kittens, Rica and Daniel, were indeed missing, as was Ariana. Talking to various Shifter teens in town revealed some fear and anger, but little information.

The trio also confirmed that no one had as yet gone to the police, in case the kids were actually in animal form somewhere and would turn up unharmed, a situation impossible to explain to the authorities. She was relieved to confirm that the abductees weren't all female, for serial killers had become all too common in recent years.

From what Codi could recall about previous killers on the news, they seemed to focus on all-male or all-female victims, so she was hoping that meant that this wasn't what they were dealing with here. She didn't even mention the possibility to the raccoon Shifters, who were worried enough already.

Still, the fact that all of the missing children were Shifters was actually even more worrisome. If the kids hadn't simply taken off, and cell phones left behind seemed to suggest that they hadn't, that meant they might indeed have been kidnapped. Since only another Shifter would have recognized his victims for what they were, that meant a Shifter gone very, very bad.

What could anyone hope to gain by kidnapping Shifter kids? The very few people who had discovered their secret had so far never been believed, so fame was out of the question.

There were certainly rich Shifters, like Teesha and Tosha whose clothes bore names like Oldham and Fiorucci, but the children who were missing certainly didn't appear to be. No ransom notes had been received, anyway.

They weren't able to track down the stranger, either. No one they talked to had met him, so Codi and Nadeem ended up not even being sure if the man was still in town. And they couldn't go to the police.

Finally, when the sun was getting low in the sky, the Codi and Nadeem friends left Rashda in the apartment she shared with Nadeem for the summer and hopped on Codi's motorbike to head for Strykers' territory.

After leaving the bike a safe distance away, Codi and Nadeem walked toward the gang headquarters.

When they were standing across the street, Codi quietly called the crow girls' names, hoping Teesha and Tosha heard her before some gang member did.

Fortunately, a moment later the birds appeared at the roof edge, and Codi gestured back toward the place they'd parked the bike. She hadn't seen the girls' car, and she didn't know if they'd parked it somewhere else to be less conspicuous, or whether they had taken the bus here to avoid any risk to their expensive vehicle.

The birds bobbed their heads in agreement, and Codi and Nadeem turned and walked quickly but casually away from the building. They met the girls coming out of an alley a bit further up the street than the time before.

"Code, my girl, back to check on our little Pookster, are ya?" said Teesha —unless they'd switched beads, in which case it was Tosha.

"Hey, Nadeem, ya cute thang, howya doin'?" the other girl asked.

Codi didn't wanted to embarrass herself by calling the girls by the wrong names, but Nadeem didn't seem to have the same problem. "Hey, Teesh," he said in his quiet voice, shaking hands with the green-beaded girl. Codi made a mental note to ask Nadeem how he told them apart.

"'Deem," said the blue-beaded girl, holding Nadeem's hand long enough that Codi could see the raccoon blush even beneath his dusky skin. "Codi drag you out here to see Pook, or us?"

"You, I – I think," stammered Nadeem. The raccoon Shifter could usually gab up a storm, but he was a bit shy with girls, particularly such pretty ones as these. Then, seeming to need to make small talk before broaching the more serious subject he said, "How's college?"

"Well, we survived freshman year," said Tosha. She had by now let go of Nadeem's hand, but was smiling a heart-quickening smile all the same.

"Wish I didn't have to start college in a few weeks," said Nadeem, an outright lie as Codi well knew, for Nadeem was a nerd who truly seemed to love school. Codi would never understand that. She herself still wasn't sure about starting college in a few weeks, despite her parents' pressure. Since all she wanted was to be a drummer, what more was there for her to learn?

"So, like, what can we do for you?" said Teesha a little too loudly, perhaps to draw the raccoon's attention back to her. Codi had never really thought much about Nadeem's looks, but she noted now, reflected in the girls' interest, that the raccoon Shifter was actually quite handsome. Shiny dark hair and large brown eyes with abundant lashes. Skin the color of cinnamon-flavored cafe-au-lait. A bit chubby, actually, but who ever saw a skinny raccoon? Though she had never thought of him in any way except as a tutor, Codi felt a pang of jealousy that Nadeem was attracting other female attention.

She quickly suppressed the feeling. They were here on business, even if it appeared Nadeem had for the moment completely forgotten his missing girlfriend.

As if he'd heard her thoughts, Nadeem gathered his wits with a visible effort and answered Teesha's question, his round face returning to its worried expression. "A number of Testing Shifter kids have disappeared over the past week or so. Heard anything about it?"

The two girls look at each other for a moment, obviously aghast. "Not a peep," said Teesha.

"Been focusing on the rabbit over there involved with this gang," said Tosha, tilting her head toward the warehouse. "Why? Who's missing?"

"As far as we know, two older kittens and a cardinal named Ariana."

"Oh, man, that's horrible," said Tosha. Both girls knew Ariana from school as well. "Do you know what happened to 'em?"

Codi shrugged unhappily. "Not really. We've been all over town, talking to other Shifters. All we know is they were all Testing this summer. Nadeem here is convinced they've been kidnapped, but I think it's possible they've just taken off somewhere for a few days."

Nadeem shot Codi an angry look. "The evidence suggests they didn't leave voluntarily. They didn't take any of their personal stuff with them – cell phones, purses, whatever. They seem to have just disappeared. And before you ask, I'm, uh, Ariana's boyfriend, so I don't think she's run off with someone."

"Chill, dude, I wasn't even goin' there," said Teesha.

She looked over at her cousin. "Guess it's time we left the bunny to fend for herself for awhile, and asked a few questions 'round town ourselves."

"Great," said Codi. "I was hoping you'd help out. You can cover territory faster than either of us, and I figure you probably have sources we don't. One more thing. I've been told there's a new Shifter in town from South America who may or may not be involved. Heard of him?"

Again the girls looked at each other as if communing telepathically, and both shrugged. "Nope," said Tosha. "We're totally out of the loop on this one. We'll check him out, too, if we can. Come on, cuz, we better get goin'. There's only 'bout an hour of sunlight left."

"Maybe we should fly from here," Teesha said, looking very serious. "Can either of you drive a car?"

"I can," said Nadeem, to Codi's surprise. Codi only had her motorcycle license, and Nadeem had taken the bus when he was tutoring her.

Looking at Codi, Nadeem added in explanation, "Mom and Dad made me do Defensive Driving as soon as school was out. At the end of the course, we had the option of using the company's car to do our driver's test, so I got my license then."

"Perfect," said Teesha, handing Nadeem the keys as the four of them walked to where the girls had hidden the car. Tosha grabbed a piece of paper and a pen from the glove compartment and gave Nadeem overly-explicit instructions on how to get to their apartment building, which turned out to be fairly close to Nadeem's place.

In return, Nadeem gave the girls his work and home phone numbers, so they could tell him if they found anything out. Codi followed Nadeem back through the city while the crows flew on ahead.

"Thanks, Codi," said Nadeem as they walked toward Codi's motorbike after they had left the girls' keys with the building's concierge.

"For what? We're no further ahead than we were yesterday." Codi was tired and discouraged. Bad enough to be made to feel responsible for a girl involved with a gang; Codi was completely unprepared to deal with missing children. What if they didn't find them? What if they were dead? Her days of snoozing on warm rocky ledges in the forest seemed a lifetime away.

"It's okay, Codi," said Nadeem, whose face said it wasn't okay. "We're doing all we can."

"If you really believe that the kids are in danger, don't you think we should get adult Shifters involved? I hate the thought of ruining the kids' Tests if it turns out they've simply run off together to someone's cottage, or whatever, but if you're right ..."

"For now, no adults," said Nadeem. "Too soon to go running for help. We don't actually know if anything bad has happened or not. I know I'd be very angry if someone spoiled my Test that way."

"I'll keep eyes and ears open, though I don't really talk to people much," admitted Codi when they stood in front of house where Nadeem and Rashda had a second-floor apartment. Then she looked closely at the raccoon Shifter, who looked stressed out. "Anything else I can do? You're making yourself crazy."

"No, thank you ... I might as well go in to work tomorrow. It won't do me any good hanging around home worrying, and we've done all the searching I can think to do."

Nadeem worked at a computer store (so cliché!), and Codi vacillated between envy at the extra money the guy was making with a full-time job for the summer, and gratitude that she only had to work two evenings a week to survive, leaving her free to live in her beloved forest the rest of the week.

Since he was planning to attend college in the fall – something to do with information technology, whatever that was, which he had explained more than once, and which Codi didn't understand any better than she had the first time – it was important for Nadeem that, by the end of summer, he had saved for tuition and wouldn't have to take out a student loan.

"Okay," Codi said at last. "Going to work is probably the best thing to do. Teesha and Tosha will get in touch with you the minute they know something ... I guess I'll go back to the forest in the morning. I'll ask around with the Shifters I know out there to see if they've heard anything about either the missing kids or the stranger, and I'll check in with you on Saturday when I return to play with the band. Okay?"

"Sounds good, Codi ... Thanks."

They shook hands in their special way again, and then Codi headed to her apartment. When she got there, though, it felt too quiet. The Gardiners must have been out, and for once she missed the small talk.

Finally, she made up her mind, got back on her bike, and drove out to the state park. She locked the motorcycle in the maintenance shed and shifted to coyote. She was still a fair ways from her den, though, and since she was tired before she started, it was late when she finally arrived at her forest home.

She sat outside her den in the moonlight, exhausted, listening to other coyotes howling. For a moment she considered joining in. She was convinced these sessions were where she'd learned to sing, where she'd learned to love music. To her ears, coyotes howling in the night was a kind of eerily-beautiful music humans never even approximated.

But tonight, she was too tired in body and spirit to sing along. She felt she had aged ten years in the last day. It seemed impossible that it was only weeks ago she had insisted on Testing this summer so she could have her independence. She had felt ready for adulthood. Right now, she wished she could snuggle up to her mom and dad like she had done when she was a pup, when responsibilities were their problem rather than hers, when the biggest thing she had to worry about was learning to hunt grasshoppers.

She had been so certain that adulthood equaled freedom. Paying her own bills had been kind of fun over the past month. It had been very satisfying to eat food you'd earned with your own labor or hunted with your own skills.

However, she would have given anything right now to be able to ask their advice, to hand this problem – these problems, if you counted the rabbit – over to them to deal with while she got on with making music and sleeping the summer away.

She sighed as she turned to enter her den. After sniffing carefully to make sure no badger or other unwelcome visitor was waiting for her, Codi trod wearily down the path to the bottom. She dug for a moment to expose cool clay to lie on, for the nights had not yet begun to get colder, though with only a few weeks left in August, autumn should be on its way.

Despite how tired she felt, sleep was a long time coming. She worried about Pook, not liking how rough that ganger boy had been with her. She worried about Ariana and the other missing children. What else could go wrong?

Chapter Three:

Early the next morning, Codi was shaken out of her sleep by sounds she couldn't at first identify. Rising to her feet, she forced her weary legs up to the entrance of the den.

Her large ears rotated like radar dishes, and she panted to taste the wind that whistled through the pines. The hackles along the back of her neck and shoulders stood on end in response to a danger she hadn't yet isolated.

Gunshots! What the –? This was a state park. Hunting wasn't allowed here, period. What was going on? She crept out into the forest in the direction of the sound. It was barely dawn, and she was grateful for the deep shadows which hid her. She had never seen or smelled a ranger in the forest this early in the morning. It had to be poachers.

It hadn't happened in her lifetime, but her parents told stories of poachers who came into the forest to take deer and other small game when they thought no one was around.

Codi could hardly believe her bad luck, even as more shots rang out, ahead and to the right, deeper into the woods. As if she didn't already have enough on her plate!

She crept forward cautiously. Every animal within miles must have been frightened off by now. What could there possibly be left to shoot at? Still, she felt she had to check it out. Maybe this was related to the missing kids! She had to know if another Shifter had been injured or killed.

First she smelled the acrid smoke of guns, then the disgusting scent of unwashed male humans. And – What??

There was also a male Shifter doing the hunting! So Nadeem and Rashda had been right! Codi hesitated, hearing her father's voice in her mind: "Coyotes mind their own business, and stay out of other people's. We survive in just about every country of the world by being invisible. Strength in Solitude."

She couldn't remember either of her parents ever helping anyone. Not that they were bad people, she reasoned, just not – joiners. It was not The Coyote Way. Neither of them had ever wanted to be in a band, either. She knew her father wouldn't understand or approve of what she was about to do any more than he did Codi's love of Latin music.

Careful to stay downwind and out of sight in case they had a dog, Codi crawled forward on her belly until she could see the hunter's legs. There were three sets of them, all wearing jeans and work boots. She couldn't tell which one was the Shifter because they stood so close together, and she couldn't see what was beyond them. They didn't seem to have a dog with them, fortunately, so she decided she didn't have to stay downwind and risked circling around, careful not to make a sound.

The men weren't so careful. "Ya see it?" asked one.

"Nah," said another. "It's gotta be around here somewheres, though ... How many more of these freaks do we gotta get, boss? We got half a dozen already."

"Jou weell be sileent and do has I tell jou," said a male voice with a heavy Spanish accent. "We weell find thee small deer and get out before thee park poleez arrive. Thee number eez none of jour concern." Then he laughed, a laugh without a shred of humor. "We need quite a beeg collection. Remember! The more deers, the more dineros!"

The hair on Codi's neck stood on end. This had to be the rogue Shifter! His voice held a menace unlike anything Codi had ever heard.

It was the voice of cold steel, the voice of someone with no conscience, no feeling for the suffering of others. Codi trembled as she thought of Shifter kids at the mercy of this monster. She had to do something!

The hunters had begun moving forward, swiping at the bushes with the butts of their rifles, looking for something, and complaining under their breaths about the mosquitoes, which were attracted to their warmth in the early-morning chill.

Codi suddenly realized they were searching for whatever it was they had shot. She had to act fast, especially if this was another Shifter victim. As quietly as she could, she raced around and into the bushes ahead of them. She tried not to think of the danger she was putting herself in.

She smelled their quarry before she saw it. In the middle of the thick undergrowth, a fawn was lying on her side, panting. At least she wasn't dead. Codi approached cautiously. Shifter, all right. One of the reasons Shifters lived so long was that their ability to shift from animal to human and back offered them the opportunity to reject injured flesh in transition, and Codi wondered why this Shifter wasn't doing so.

She could smell, but not see, the fawn's parents close by. Shifter deer were just as timid as their animal counterparts, so it wasn't surprising the adults had chosen to remain hiding rather than challenge the hunters – in deer or human form.

Once she was up close, Codi saw the reason the fawn wasn't shifting. She hadn't been shot with a bullet, but rather a dart of some kind. She was unconscious. So. The hunters must be hoping to take her alive!

For a moment, Codi allowed herself to feel relief the other Shifter kids apparently hadn't been killed. They might be all right! Then she remembered the ugliness of the rogue Shifter's voice, and she was more afraid than ever. She had to lead the hunters away from the fawn to give her a chance to escape.

So after nudging the fawn with her nose to make sure she wouldn't awaken and reveal her location, Codi turned to slip through the trees. When she caught sight of the three men, and against her better judgment, she flashed her tawny coat and bushy tail in their faces and ran away.

"Another one!" shouted someone, but Codi couldn't tell if it was the rogue Shifter because she was too busy running. She heard the crack of a gun, and felt something graze her back as she twisted in the air. Fortunately, the shot hadn't hit her squarely, and she heard the dart hit the ground in the direction she'd been heading a moment before.

She knew every inch of the forest, so she knew where she wanted to go. She heard them running after her as she streaked along a deer path through the undergrowth. Their human instincts would cause them to stick to the path, which twisted and turned enough they wouldn't be able to get a clear shot at her.

As she emerged from the bushes a moment later, she heard them shouting and cursing, and knew she had a moment to catch her breath, for they had run straight into wild blackberry bushes, full of thorns, which hung across the path.

By the time the hunters were in sight again, their bare arms bloody, Codi was sitting on the edge of a ravine a hundred yards away, saucily licking her fur like a cat. They don't call coyote the Trickster for nothing, she smiled to herself. That had been a most excellent prank!

As the hunters drew nearer, however, every instinct urged her to escape, but she couldn't afford to lose them until they were far enough from the fawn that they'd never be able to double back and find her.

"Get heem!" shouted one of the men, and while thinking, "So sexist!", Codi leapt down the slope just as a gun boomed. The hillside was lined with moss-covered rocks which Codi nimbly sprinted across.

Hiding behind a large boulder, she turned to see the three hunters sliding down the steep embankment, grabbing small trees to prevent themselves from falling, their guns hanging uselessly from shoulder straps. She allowed herself a coyote grin as she trotted in full view across the stream at the bottom of the ravine. It was just wide enough that the hunters wouldn't be able to jump across to avoid getting their feet wet.

She followed the riverbank for a few moments until she came to a hollow log, a tempting hiding place. But the hunters were already swearing as they splashed their way across the water, so she didn't have time for hide 'n' seek.

Instead, she looked back over her shoulder to make sure they saw her, and then darted into the woods at the end of the ravine.

Codi allowed herself to get far enough ahead to double back and lie atop a rocky cliff and get a good look at them as they went by. All she could see was the tops of their heads and their retreating backs, but that was enough to tell her they were all big, even the rogue Shifter – big enough that in Codi's human form, they could probably break her like a twig. She shuddered.

Pushing her fear aside, she circled ahead and brought herself back into view for a split second, then once more led them away from the unconscious fawn. There was a hiking path up ahead that she knew would be irresistible to the tired, wet, scratched-up hunters. When she heard them slowing down, though, she looped back and raced to a nearby clearing, taunting them with a moment's view of her laughing face before she turned and leapt away. She heard another gunshot and a dart brushed the tips of her whiskers before embedding itself in a tree trunk just inches from her body. Her stomach clenched in fear.

Much as she wanted to help the fawn, she didn't want to be among the missing, either. Fortunately, the hunters were already tiring. All she had to do was keep leading them away without getting shot. Easy, right? She wondered how long her luck would last.

She raced ahead in the lightening shadows, following the edge of the hiking path until she was just a hundred yards from the parking lot. She could hear the men behind her, though she didn't take the time to look back, and thought her luck might be holding after all.

She didn't dare cross the open space of the lot, but perhaps leading her enemies here should be sufficient discouragement from going back through the entire forest to search for the fawn. It was a risk she had to take.

She was mere yards away from the parking lot when something made her turn her head. She found herself looking right at the barrel-chested Shifter, who had obviously guessed Codi's next move and was waiting for her with his gun ready to fire. It seemed Carmen had been right to fear for the missing kids. Beneath a shock of silver-streaked hair, the man's dark eyes burned with menace. Out of the sleeves of a dirty t-shirt bulged biceps as big around as Codi's thighs. He was smiling, an evil smile that froze Codi with a new kind of terror for one second too long.

Too late, she turned to flee. 'Bang!' There was a stinging in her rump, and she only had time to slip once again into the undergrowth before she felt darkness creeping over her. As her legs gave out, she cursed her own cockiness. Now she and the fawn would both be captives! Then she heard a scream, and everything went black.

***

When she came to, she was lying under a blanket of some kind. A girl was looking at her with worry and affection, and for a groggy moment Codi thought she was with the missing children.

"Mom, she's awake!" the girl cried shrilly, making Codi's head ache.

As the girl turned away to call again, Codi shifted to human form, struggled to sit up, and a dizzy moment later found a motherly arm helping her.

"Are you okay?" the woman asked with a worried voice. A statuesque blonde, she wasn't Ariana, that was for sure.

Codi's head felt like it had been hit with a hammer, and when she tried to turn her head to look around, things went black before her eyes. She struggled to remain conscious. She felt like she was behind a glass wall, the voices around her coming as if from a great distance. What had happened?

"I'm okay, I guess. Where ... am I?" she mumbled, her lips feeling thick and numb.

"In the forest. D'uh," said the brown-eyed girl, as if Codi were an idiot.

"Shhh," her mother cautioned. "Lana, remember, she saved your life, so you'd better be nice to her."

"You – you're the fawn?" Codi asked. "But – but I failed, the hunter shot me, and ..."

"My husband followed you to make sure the hunters didn't get you, after you were so brave in leading them away from our daughter," the woman said. "He charged the hunter and knocked him down. The other hunters grabbed the man and jumped into their truck and left. Dieter can be pretty scary when he's mad."

"Good. Uh ... so everyone is okay?" It was beginning to come back to her. The saucy race through the forest, leading the men away from the helpless fawn. Her confidence that she had led them a merry dance, and then ... the eyes of the Shifter hunter, crazed with hatred. The gun shot, the pain, the darkness ...

"What's your name?" Lana said before her mother could answer Codi's question. Her voice was either very high-pitched, or else the drug was making Codi hyper-sensitive to sound. Every word the girl spoke stabbed Codi behind the eyes.

She winced, but forced herself to answer. "Codi," she said, extending her hand. "Pleased to meet ... Lana ... glad you're okay ... glad I'm okay, too."

She turned carefully toward the woman, extending her hand to her in turn. "You are? – How's your husband?"

"My name's Hyacinth," said the woman quietly as she shook her hand. She must have noticed how Lana's voice hurt her. "My husband Dieter is fine. He's off somewhere, guarding us he says, but really just working off steam, I think. I shudder to think what would have happened to Lana if not for your quick action. I – We're embarrassed that we didn't think of leading the hunters away ourselves, in the shock of seeing our girl shot. Technically, we shouldn't even have been keeping an eye on her, since she's Testing this summer, but every few days we've been coming by to make sure she's okay. Since we don't help her in any way, we figured we're not interfering enough to make her fail." Hyacinth looked embarrassed, as did Lana. Codi's groggy mind had a hard time following the long speech, but she thought she'd got the gist of it.

"I'm glad you did," said the girl, hugging her mom. "I don't care if I do fail. And thank you again for your bravery," she said, smiling shyly at Codi.

Codi smiled back wanly. "Looks like your dad returned the favor awfully fast." She wanted to stand up, but her legs wouldn't co-operate.

"Glad to be of service," said a deep male voice, and Codi turned slowly to see a tall, wide-shouldered, fair-haired man emerge from the woods with a quiet dignity.

He approached her and extended his hand. "Dieter, pleased to meet you."

Hyacinth helped Codi stand up, still a bit shaky as she reached out to grip the man's hand. "Codi. Thank you for saving me from the hunters."

"It was the least I could do," said Dieter. He nodded at her daughter. "I see you've met our scamp?"

"Da-ad," complained Lana, moving nonetheless into the protective curve of his arm. "I've already introduced myself to Codi."

"Very good," said Dieter. "Are you okay now, Codi?"

"I'm better than I would have been if you hadn't intervened ... What happened to the hunter who shot me? I thought I heard him scream before I went under."

"I rammed him with my fine set of antlers," said Dieter proudly, rubbing the top of his head as if feeling for them.

"Did you – kill him?"

"Unfortunately not," said Dieter. "He fell, but his friends helped him up. I was a short distance away, hiding from their guns. They helped him back to their truck. I was glad they either didn't know he'd hit you, or didn't take the time to find you before they left."

"Me too," said Codi. She was silent for a moment, thinking about how close she had come to joining the missing kids. Then another thought struck her, and she winced.

"What's wrong?" asked Hyacinth anxiously. "Do you hurt somewhere?"

"No, it's just that it has occurred to me that if I had let them take me, I'd at least know where the other captives are."

"Other captives?" all three deer asked at once.

After retreating farther into the safety of the woods, Codi sat down with them and explained about the kidnappings, and how one of the hunters was also a Shifter.

"This is terrible," said Dieter with a very serious face. "I should have sensed that one of the hunters was a Shifter, but I was too preoccupied worrying about my daughter. I thought they were poachers, at least until I saw the tranquilizer dart." Codi saw the pain in his eyes.

" Then I didn't know what to think, except that my child was on the ground, unconscious," Dieter continued. "And then you – well, thank you again for your quick thinking and courage."

The tall man hesitated. "As for the other kidnapped children, I don't know what to say."

"I got the impression they're 'collecting' a number of Shifter kids. I just don't know why, or where they're keeping them."

"So we must find out where they are."

"I realize that if they'd taken me, I'd simply be a captive, too," began Codi. "What we really need to do is to somehow follow them back to where they're keeping the children." She wasn't able to stifle a yawn.

"You go sleep for a few hours," said Hyacinth immediately. "We will check with some of the other Shifters in the area, and see if we can come up with a plan."

Codi couldn't think of a better idea, so she reluctantly agreed. The deer politely turned their backs while she shifted back into coyote. After thanking her a final time, the deer family waved goodbye and she left for her den. They had agreed to meet that night by a large pond far from any human paths.

* * *

Codi awoke in darkness, not knowing where she was, or what time it was. She reached for the bedroom lamp to turn it on ... and felt her paw strike a hard dirt wall. Oh. A coyote. Yes. As she lifted her head to get up, a wave of dizziness swept over her, and for a few minutes she lay panting, trying hard not to puke in her den.

If she did, the stench would stick around for months. She'd have to move. Finally, she was able to stand without falling, and carefully crept to the entrance.

The cool evening air helped clear her head, and she began to feel better. Starving hungry, too. In the faint glow of moonlight on her way to the rendezvous, Codi struggled to catch some mice for dinner, one of the staples of her diet. The necessary sudden lunges were excruciating, however, and she gave up with her stomach far from full. Not only that, but despite the fact that she was normally quite comfortable with the darkness, and maybe because her reflexes were impaired or because she was still in shock from being shot, Codi found herself walking stiff-legged with fear. Every sound and movement in the corner of her eyes made her start, her heart pounding. She realized she had never been in danger, real danger, until this week, and found she wasn't as brave as she'd thought she was.

When she reached the pond, it appeared deserted. She was neither surprised nor worried by this. In their animal forms, Shifters didn't exactly wear watches. While she waited, still in coyote form, she discovered some ripe blackberries, and feasted on the sweet, juicy fruit until she felt she could eat no more. Better than donuts any time! She trotted cautiously to the water's edge to lap the cool, clear water.

Satisfied, she found a small bush to hide in and shifted to her human form. She had no sooner finished when she heard a noise from behind her. Suddenly worried about the return of the hunters despite her previous confidence that they wouldn't come here at night, she crouched down, cursing her weak human hearing as she sought the origin of the sound.

To her surprise, four young Shifters emerged from various directions around the pond. A skunk and two mice that she didn't know, and Nadeem. She was a bit confused. What was Nadeem doing here? Then an owl floated down out of the sky just as Codi stepped out of the bush she'd been hiding in and found a fallen log to sit on. She waited silently while they all Shifted to human and joined her.

"Hi, Codi," said Nadeem. "The deer got word to the city about this pow-wow." He turned to the other Shifters. "I'm Nadeem. Nice to meet you ..." Nadeem directed an embarrassed smile at the owl-girl, who wore round Harry Potter glasses with thick lenses that magnified her eyes so that she did indeed look quite owlish.

"Hi, Nadeem," Codi said. She glanced over at the others. "I'm Codi ... Are you here about the missing kids?"

"Whoooo?" said the owl-girl, who flashed a quick smile to show she was kidding. "Sorry, can never resist that the first time I meet someone. Name's Tavia. Here to help, if I can." She was even shorter than Codi, but had a nice smile. She looked about sixteen.

"Peter," said the skunk, a skinny black kid with a white streak in his dark hair, who looked fifteen at most. "Count me in."

"Derek and Deena," said the mice at the same time. They looked at each other and smiled. "Twins," they added together, unnecessarily. "We'll do anything we can." They were small enough to be jockeys, thought Codi, and younger than the others, looking maybe fourteen in human years.

"Codi, Nadeem has volunteered to be the next 'victim' of the kidnappers," Tavia said.

"What? You've got to be kidding!" She looked back at Nadeem, who was nodding vigorously.

"Yep," said Nadeem, "that's the plan. We figure that when the hunters return, which we think will be soon unless the rogue Shifter is more injured than Dieter thought, I'll just happen to be the first Shifter they come across. Boom! I'm kidnapped."

"Nadeem, that's very brave of you," began Codi, but Nadeem cut her off.

"No, here's the great part. We get those crow chicks to tail the perps back to their lair, and then come back and tell you and Tavia, Peter, and the D's, who swoop in and sha-bam! We nail those mothers."

This was a side to the raccoon that Codi had never seen before. She thought Nadeem had seen a few too many TV cop shows, but the basic plan wasn't all that bad. She still had a question, though. "So how did you get volunteered to be the one who's going to be captured?"

"Hyacinth and the others have been roaming the forest all afternoon, looking for volunteers. Either the Shifters around here are too old, since the hunters seem to be focusing on children, or else they're too young, not old enough to take on this responsibility," Nadeem replied, showing, Codi thought, an amazing amount of common sense. She shifted her evaluation of the raccoon up a notch. Maybe two notches.

"That's very brave of you, Nadeem," she repeated thoughtfully a moment later, "but I'm not sure you realize how dangerous this could be. I don't know if Dieter or her family got a good look at the rogue Shifter, but I did, and he's scary. He looks vicious, and is probably nuts.

I'd like to believe the other Shifter kids are being held safe somewhere, but for all we know this monster is using them to experiment on." She didn't want to lose a volunteer, but felt it only fair to make the risks clear.

Nadeem's proud smile had faded as Codi spoke, and for a moment, Codi was afraid she'd said too much.

It was actually a pretty good plan, and if Nadeem backed out … well, realistically, she, Codi, was the next most likely candidate. She found it hard to swallow as she watched Nadeem's face.

Finally, though, Nadeem seemed to come to a decision. "No problemo, pardner," he said in a John Wayne voice. "We'll have those doggies rounded up and in the corral before sundown, uh-huh."

Everyone laughed, breaking the tension of the moment.

"So why the rest of you?" Codi had to ask.

"We heard it was Testing kids who'd gone missing, and no one wants to ruin their test for them. So we figured the best plan is to use other kids to at least find out where they are, and if they're really kidnapped or okay of whatever, then to get adults involved if it looks complicated or dangerous. You know?" Nadeem was nearly breathless.

"That sort of makes sense," said Codi, "but –"

"It's decided," said Tavia. "We're the front line. Nadeem here gets kidnapped, your crow friends follow the hunters to their hideaway if it's daytime, and I'll do it if it's in the night. Once we know where they are keeping the kids, we'll make more plans. Solid?"

"Yeah, sounds good," Codi said, though she wasn't entirely convinced.

The group discussed details for a long time. It was agreed lookouts were needed. Other birds would be enlisted in this capacity. Nadeem would hang out in the general vicinity of the parking lot. He said he could even spend time digging around in the garbage barrel there, a suggestion no one bothered to comment on, though secretly everyone thought he would probably enjoy it. Raccoons were notorious garbage-eaters.

The rest of the Shifters, particularly those who were Testing, or those with children, would be warned to head out to the farthest reaches of the park and stay there until the hunters were stopped.

"It might be days, or even weeks, before the hunters come back," said Codi as they were wrapping up. "I'll go into the city tonight and contact Teesha and Tosha to see if they're willing to be part of the plan. If they are, they'll have to come back to live in the forest until something happens."

She paused, smiling as she thought about how the prissy city-girls would feel about living in the forest, even temporarily. Then she got serious again. "You make sure all of the Shifters in the forest keep their kids hidden, and tell them what the hunters look like, just in case someone sees them before they come back here. Maybe we won't have to use you as bait, Nadeem."

"I'll try not to be too hurt if that's what happens," said Nadeem, smiling.

"I'll move somewhere closer to the parking lot to keep an eye on Nadeem and make sure the crow girls or Tavia know when or if the hunters strike. Okay, I guess that's it. Any questions?" finished Codi.

Everyone seemed satisfied with the plans, so the meeting broke up, and Codi headed back to the city. It was nearly morning when she finally drove her motorbike up beside the house and got off. She opened her door as quietly as possible, not wanting to frighten the Gardiners.

She'd find the crow girls in a few hours and enlist their help. It felt strangely good to be part of this, though being part of a group other than family had never interested Codi before. Still, the rogue Shifter's vicious face floated before Codi as she lay in bed trying to get to sleep.

She decided not to tell any of them exactly how crazy and dangerous the man appeared. They were already worried enough about the missing kids. Codi didn't want to make it any worse.

After only an hour or so of sleep, Codi found herself awake again, for once glad that she hadn't slept in, though she felt kind of groggy.

She called the cell number for Tosha and asked to meet with them, refusing to explain in advance. "I'll tell you when I see you, okay?"

"Okay, Miss Mysterious," said Tosha. "See you in a bit."

When Codi met with the crow girls at a coffee shop an hour later, they told her Pook seemed to be okay. "Did you find out anything more about the missing kids?" she asked when they were done telling her about Pook.

"Oh, girl," said Tosha in the saddest voice.

"What now?"

"Another one went missing yesterday afternoon," said Teesha. "Squirrel over on Third. Named Kiley."

Codi's heart sank. She had been hoping the rogue Shifter had been injured badly enough by Dieter to take a few days off. Apparently not. "Oh God," she said. "We have got to do something. This simply can't continue."

"You're right, Code ... You mentioned somethin' 'bout a plan on the phone this mornin'? What's up with that?" Teesha asked.

Codi outlined the basics, which the girls seemed to approve of for the most part.

"Brave little nerd, that Nadeem," said Tosha.

"But the idea of you hangin' out in the forest is, like, not good," said Teesha. "If we find this guy and he's in or near the city, it might take too long to go getcha. Better you stay here where we can find ya fast, ya know?"

"You're right," Codi said thoughtfully. "But what if he's holding them further out of town that way?"

"Hmmm. We better have a 'tingency plan for that, too. Why doncha have that skunk dude – Peter? – do what you were plannin' to do, hang out with Nadeem till he's caught? That way, we can, like, tell him insteada you if we hafta," said Teesha.

Codi realized she wasn't that good at planning. None of this had occurred to her. Well, she told herself, I'm the musician type, not the accountant type. I don't like planning. Still, it was a bit embarrassing how dependent she was on everyone else. Independence was supposed to be the name of the game this summer, but things seemed to be turning out quite differently.

Another thought crossed her mind. "Are you two sure you're okay with the idea of hanging out in the forest? I know you're not exactly 'outdoorsy' types. You're okay with it?"

"Not!" admitted Teesha with one of her warm smiles. Codi's wanted to keep feeling annoyed with the crows, but it was getting harder and harder. She wasn't starting to like them, was she?

"Yeah, it's not our bag, that's for sure," said Tosha. "But this is, like, an emergency. An' if those hunters were out in the woods yesterday huntin' wild Shifters, you can bet your butt they'll try it again. Like, soon."

"You're probably right. So, when are you going?"

"Just as soon as we can, like, park the car back at home," said Teesha. "Right, cuz?"

"Yep," said Tosha. "It ain't like we're gonna be needin' our extra shoes on this job. What are you, like, gonna do now?"

"I guess I'll go home and try to get a bit more sleep than I got last night. You know where to find me… except Friday and Saturday nights, when I work at the 'Baile Loco' – that's Spanish for 'Dance Crazy' – a Latin dance club, Twelfth and Jarvis. I'm there from eight on."

"You? What's a little white-bread girl like you doin' at a Latin dance club?" said Tosha in surprise. "No insult intended," she added, looking embarrassed.

"Prob'ly, like, bartending, mixin' drinks way too strong to try to get those hot Spanish dudes drunk enough to kiss 'er," said Teesha.

Codi blushed furiously at the thought of kissing Enrique, but she pushed the thought away. She didn't feel like explaining what she did at the club, either. "Something like that," she said.

"Okay, then, we know where ta find ya," said Tosha, who seemed more than willing to drop the subject.

"Thanks for meeting me," Codi said when she'd seen them to their car. "See you soon. Be safe, okay?"

"The safest," both girls said at once, then looked at each other and laughed. "Bye."

"Bye." Codi felt kind of lost as she watched the car drive away. I guess that's what happens when you face adversity together, she thought. You bond. And with the most unlikely people, too! Dad never mentioned this when he talked about 'strength in solitude'.

She wondered if her dad had ever heard the saying, 'Safety in numbers". She turned to go home, glad they had a plan but sad she didn't have better news for Nadeem.

Chapter Four:

The rest of the week was almost unnervingly uneventful. Codi stayed in her apartment, trying to be on full alert for the imminent arrival of the crow girls, who had agreed to take turns acting as trackers. Codi had hoped to catch up on her rest, but found it hard to sleep even a normal amount of time. She was too worried and anxious.

She got to talk to the Gardiners more than she ever had, though, and was even forced to expand her cooking abilities beyond scrambled eggs, KD, and spaghetti. She had been tempted to buy frozen dinners, but decided that wouldn't teach her anything new, nor use up any of the time that was moving too slowly.

So she asked Mrs. Gardiner for an easy recipe or two, and made a short, nervous visit to the local market to purchase fresh chicken, a steak, some potatoes and other vegetables. She was afraid to be somewhere the girls couldn't find her, even for half an hour. Standing in line at the checkout, Codi wondered how her life had gone from the carefree serenity of her forest summer into the current nightmare of hunters and missing children. Part of her thought that the whole thing was none of her business.

She knew that's what her dad would say, if he'd been there. But then she looked at a young girl ahead of her in line, with a sweet innocent face and short stubby legs, and decided that since she was on her own for the summer, she'd have to do what she thought was right, not what her parents might think was right. Whether it was The Coyote Way or not.

Mr. Gardiner had expressed shock that a girl her age had never tasted steak in her life. "I thought steak, baked potato, and salad were the mainstay of the single person's diet," he'd said.

She couldn't explain that to her parents, buying and cooking food was not only a needless expense, but made them more 'human' than they wanted to be.

Even when they were staying mostly in the city during the school year, all three of them had shifted to coyotes nightly in the nearest park to hunt their own dinners. Her mother allowed her to take a lunch to school to 'be like the other kids', but that was as far as it went. They were coyotes first, human second. Steak was expensive anyway, and both parents worked at casual jobs – her father carpentry, her mother housecleaning – that left more of their time free but their bank accounts practically empty.

The steak Codi made wasn't bad, really, just a bit chewy. Mrs. Gardiner had said people often ate it "bloody", which actually sounded about right to her, but had warned that it was important to make sure all meat was "fully cooked".

Codi wasn't sure if there was any truth to this fear or not, suspecting that the woman's British ancestry might be more responsible than any real health dangers, if the overcooked meals she'd served Codi once or twice were any indication. Still, Codi had heeded her warning this once at least, and had cooked the steak until it was brown all the way through.

Two bites in, she decided the next steak, if there ever was one, would be more bloody than brown, that was for sure. The potatoes were good, though, especially with the liberal quantities of butter, sour cream, onion and bacon bits she'd been told to add, but she didn't really care for the salad. Coyotes were omnivorous, but vegetables were never going to be a central part of her diet.

The chicken cacciatore on Friday was better, definitely an improved way to eat spaghetti. When she was done, though, she found the amount of cookware she had to clean distressing. At least all the steak had used was a frying pan. And since the pots and pans were Mrs. Gardiner's, she didn't dare let them get crusty in the sink as she was tempted to do.

Instead, she forced herself to spend the extra half hour cleaning up, then returned the cookware upstairs with her thanks. When she came back down, she realized it was time to leave for the club.

She couldn't believe how much she was looking forward to playing. The sheer physicality of standing and drumming – well, actually dancing and drumming – appealed to her restless nature, and when she found herself yearning for the camaraderie of the band, she realized how lonely she'd been all week, despite her chats with the Gardiners.

It was strange. Codi hadn't missed seeing anyone, even Nadeem, who was the closest thing she had to a friend, since the summer started. She didn't recall missing her parents, either, and she'd spent most of July alone, albeit in the forest.

So she wasn't sure what to make of her sudden desire for companionship. Maybe she'd been spending too much time as a human, she decided. After the show, she was going to go coyote for a few hours, even if she had to do it in the privacy of her apartment.

It only took a few minutes to get ready to perform. She slicked her hair back with some gel, and put on the white cotton shirt and tight black pants that were the 'uniform' of the band. She slipped small gold hoops into her pierced ears, and examined herself critically in the mirror.

Very different from the shaggy-mopped 'invisible' kid she'd been in high school. Her father would not approve. "Invisible is invincible," was another of his favorite sayings.

Codi had discovered her musical talent accidentally. While other girls in ninth grade were listening to Em 'n' Em, Codi had found herself drawn to a genre she'd heard once on the radio while flipping stations to avoid commercials.

The pounding drums and love of life in Latin dance music attracted her far more than the dark, angry lyrics of her classmates' music, and soon she was spending every extra dollar to download songs from the bands she'd discovered on the Internet at school.

Then one day in the music class every ninth grader was forced to take, Codi had been nosing through the cupboards at the back of the room while waiting for the teacher, who was late. She'd come across a set of bongos, and soon found herself pounding out the rhythms of the music she listened to all the time.

When the teacher finally entered the room, Codi had a circle of admirers standing around her while she played. Codi remembered the teacher's – Mrs. Dumphries, yeah, that was her name – amazement. Codi had been a mediocre clarinet player at best. Mrs. Dumphries immediately taught her to read percussion sheet music and finally found her an inexpensive private instructor, a high school senior named Miguel, whose family were Cuban refugees. They had helped her obtain a set of used conga drums on which to practice.

Dragging her attention back to the mirror, Codi decided she looked okay. She smiled at herself for a moment, but it was the feral smile of a predator, and it faded instantly. She hoped she didn't look like that on stage.

As she walked from her apartment to the club, she thought back to her audition for the drummer job at the beginning of the previous summer. Walking into the club that day, her heart had been pounding with fear. Her high school Spanish was going to sound pretty bad, she remembered thinking, if they didn't speak English.

"Buenos días," she said to the bouncer at the door. Then her Spanish deserted her entirely, and she stammered, "I am ... um ... here to try out for the drummer job?"

"Straight to the back," said the bouncer in perfect English.

Codi had blushed with embarrassment. Of course they spoke English. They lived a thousand miles from the nearest Spanish-speaking country.

"Hi," she said to the group of young people on the stage, smiling her best 'Please like me' smile.

"Buenos días," said one of them, rolling his eyes toward the others as if to say, 'Can you believe this gringa?'.

"I'm ... uh ... here for the drumming job?"

"We're a – Latin – dance band," said one of the other boys carefully, smirking.

"Yes, I know that," said Codi, forcing herself to smile instead of getting angry at his patronizing tone. "That's what I play: quinto, conga-slash-segundo, and tumbadora." Naming all of the drums was a good start, she figured.

A few eyebrows were raised, as if amazed she knew this much. "Who do you listen to?" the tallest, best-looking guy in the group asked. "Who's hot?"

"Los Van Van, Banda Latina, Alex Torres y Los Rehes Latinos, and Section Eleven," said Codi. "I also like techno-reggae, hip-hop, and trance, but there isn't much demand for those kinds of music in this town."

The band members all laughed, and she realized she'd passed one stage of a test. "So, do you want to hear me play? I can solo, or jam with you if you'd prefer." She climbed up the steps to the stage, and extended her hand. "I'm Codi, by the way. Nice to meet you."

"Frank." "Carlos." "Julio." "Abdon." "Tim." "Ana." "Tony." Each of them shook her hand the same way: contact, swing down, let go. They were all about the same age she was, late-teens, maybe early twenties. Frank looked a little older, and was probably the boss, the way the others had looked at him when Codi asked if she should play. Codi was glad there was at least one other girl in the band, though Ana seemed to be sizing her up.

"Go solo for a minute or two first," said Frank, confirming Codi's guess about leadership. "Let's hear mambo, merengue, samba, rumba catalana, and salsa, in that order. Okay?"

"Ningún problema," said Codi, and watched their eyebrows rise again. "Demasiado fácil." She was almost certain her accent sucked, but she wanted them to know she was willing to try to fit in. Suddenly it occurred to her that only a couple of them had had Spanish accents.

Perhaps the rest had been born here and didn't speak a word of Spanish themselves. She smiled at the thought, then pushed it aside as she positioned herself behind the waist-high drums.

It took a moment and a couple of false starts while she got used to the drums, which were slightly different from the ones she had at home, but then the heart-thing happened to her, and she segued between rhythms easily, dancing to music she heard in her head.

When she stopped, she was sweating. Her freshly-pressed white shirt was damp under the arms, and a strand of hair had flopped onto her forehead.

There was a moment's silence when she wondered if she'd somehow blown it, then Frank began to clap, followed, with only a moment's hesitation, by the rest of the band. From over her shoulder, Codi heard the bartender guy clapping too, and this time, her smile was genuine.

"Thanks," she told them when they stopped. "Drumming is in my blood, I think."

"If it's not too rude to ask, are you Hispanic somewhere in your ancestry that we can't see?" laughed the boy Codi thought was named Carlos, though she'd already forgotten who was who.

"Not that I know of," smiled Codi. "My parents have actually wondered the same thing. My father says he doesn't remember a

Hispanic mailman, but there must have been one, 'cause there aren't any musicians in the family, let alone anyone obsessed with Latin dance music."

What she didn't tell them was that her father, while ultimately supportive enough to help her pay for her own drums, had been completely baffled by a daughter who wanted to be a performer.

"Coyotes don't like the limelight," her father had explained, or rather complained, Codi thought. "I don't see how you can want to stand up in front of a bunch of people who are staring at you, night after night."

Codi couldn't explain it, either. All she could say was, "I just do."

He not only didn't understand Codi's joy in performing, Codi saw her father actually look hurt when he and Codi's mom had come – once – to see their daughter play.

She knew that to her father, she was risking exposure of her Shifter self, but Codi couldn't see how a life without some risks, and especially, without this kind of joy, was worth living.

One of the many things she and her father couldn't talk about. Her mother never said much at the best of times, and when Codi and her dad were arguing, her mom usually disappeared into another room.

That night, though, the band members were laughing, and Codi had dragged her mind back to the present as Frank asked her to jam with them. It made sense; it was all very well to know the rhythms, but if you can't keep time with the rest, you'll kill the whole group.

It was hard, because she'd only ever drummed to CDs, never with a live band, and their pauses and timing were a bit different than she was used to, even though she was familiar with the songs they chose.

By the end of an hour, though, she'd gotten into the swing of it. She found she could time herself by their base player, Abdon, for the moment at least.

"What do you think, compañeros?" said Frank to the rest when they had finally stopped and gone to sit around a table with beers.

Codi had expected them to tell her she could go so they could discuss her privately. She'd been surprised to be invited to join them at the table, and was even more surprised to hear Frank talk about her as if she wasn't there.

So she was greatly relieved to see six thumbs up. She smiled her thanks, lifting her cola in salute. She put the glass down quickly, though, when Frank turned and offered her hand.

"I guess this means you're in," Frank said. "Rehearsals are Wednesday nights, we play Fridays and Saturdays. A hundred and fifty dollars a night, plus tips shared if we get any. If you're a no-show more than once, you're out of the band. Deal?"

"Um ..." said Codi, hating what she had to say. "I'm ... ah ... often out of town during the week in the summer. My parents travel for work," she said, her standard explanation, which no one seemed to question. "But if you play during the school year, I'm here all week, and I'm sure I can get a ride into town for a few weeks to get into the swing of things."

Frank looked unhappy, and Codi thought it was all over. The leader glanced at the other members of the band, who were shrugging as if leaving the decision up to him.

"Okay, here's the deal. Be here the next four Wednesday nights, so we can teach you the songs we wrote ourselves. Abdon, go get her the percussion sheets so she can start practicing at home. We'll keep the music easy for the next four Fridays and Saturdays. Our regular drummer just moved to Buffalo, so we need someone right away. After that, as long as you keep up and don't mess up, you can rehearse Wednesdays or not. How's that?"

"More than fair," Codi said, taking Frank's offered hand. "I'll be here ... Thanks," she said to Abdon who was handing her a sheaf of paper. "I'll get right on this stuff."

"Drugs, booze, guy problems?" asked the boy Codi thought was Julio.

"Are you asking or offering?" Abdon said, and everyone laughed again.

"No to all three, actually," said Codi. "I don't much like the taste of booze, and I'm not into drugs, either. Guy problems are for girls that guys are interested in, I guess."

"Wait a month," laughed Frank. "Being in a band is the best aphrodisiac I know of."

The others smiled their agreement, even Ana, and Codi had a job.

Tonight, she was looking forward to rejoining the people who had gone from being bandmates to being something as close as she got to friends.

She thought they were still a little suspicious of her non-Hispanic background, some kind of reverse prejudice she had decided not to challenge.

Her Spanish had improved immensely with the practice she got with those who spoke it, and working together, the members of the band were as warm and friendly with her as they were with each other.

But when each performance was done, no one invited her out to an after-hours club or tried to call her during the week to do other things. Until now, this situation had suited her perfectly, but tonight she couldn't help feeling a pang of envy when she saw them laughing together on the stage as she walked in the door.

Well, she told herself, I've got a 'tribe' of my own, one more strange than you could ever imagine. Thinking of how Dieter had risked his own life to save hers, how Nadeem had volunteered to be kidnapped and maybe killed to help out a bunch of kids, most of whom he didn't know, made Codi realize how lucky she really was to be a Shifter.

The evening went by in a flash, and she was drinking her cola with the other members of the band just before going on for the last set when a warm hand settled on her shoulder.

She glanced up, expecting to see a groupie hoping for some rubbed-off 'fame', and had her standard response of, 'Thanks but no thanks' already in her mouth, when she saw who it was.

Teesha, smiling at her as if she were her best friend in the world. Codi surprised herself as she leapt out of her chair to hug the crow girl.

"Sorry," she said after a second, pulling away, "I guess I'm all sweaty and stinky. What are you doing here? Not that I'm not glad to see you."

If Teesha was offended by her hug, she showed no sign. "Good to see you, too, Code. So this is where you work, huh? Nice place. What, are you, like, on a break?"

"Aren't you going to introduce us to your girlfriend?" Abdon teased. He had been the friendliest member of the band from the beginning, perhaps because they both played in the background, and they often commiserated with each other over their shyness with members of the opposite sex.

"Oh, yeah. Guys, this is my friend, not-girlfriend, Teesha," said Codi. She told Teesha their names, and the dark girl shook each person's hand with her usual warmth. Codi found herself wishing she really were as attractive as the other girl. The boys' eyes were full of admiration, and it might have been nice to have this kind of attention from time to time. Then she gave her head a shake. Stop it! she told herself. You aren't looking for a date!

Still, she was a bit annoyed when Julio held Teesha's hand for longer than necessary, eventually turning it so he could gently kiss her knuckles.

Yeah, like you don't already have half a dozen girlfriends, Codi thought resentfully. Don't you ever quit?

She needn't have worried. As cool as chocolate ice cream, Teesha said, "Very nice, very smooth. Like, practice that a lot, I guess?" – which made the rest of them laugh and Julio turn very red.

"Can I talk to you alone for a sec, Code?" Teesha said, turning her back to Julio and speaking directly to Codi.

"We're on in five," said Julio, suddenly all business.

"I'll be there," Codi responded, leading Teesha to an empty table.

"What's up?" she asked as soon as they were alone. "Hunters came tonight?"

"Naw, nothing like that. Tosha and I just decided we'd better know where to come in case we needed to. Besides, we were like, dyin' a curiosity 'bout this job a yours. I hafta say, this place don't seem to match what I thought I knew of your personality."

"Personalities tend to be more complicated than most people think," said Codi. "But I'm glad you came. You're right, it's good to know where to go, so you don't waste time. But I'm surprised you flew here at night. I thought crows weren't night creatures."

"Actually, I flew in earlier. We enlisted an owl – Tavia, do ya know 'er? – to fly in if somethin' does happen at night, which don't seem likely. Tosha's gonna do a flyby with her to your place and this place at dawn when I, like, get back, so she'll know where to go."

Watching Teesha's face while she spoke, Codi suddenly realized she'd known it was her rather than Tosha the moment she'd seen her, despite the fact that her beads were multicolored tonight. What was it? She couldn't put her finger on it. She had avoided both girls all during school, so she'd never gotten to know them well enough to tell apart, she decided.

But they definitely weren't identical, beads or no beads. "Sounds like a good plan," she said finally, to cover up the fact she'd been staring at the other girl. "Um ... It looks like I need to go now. You're welcome to stay if you want."

"Yeah, I'll hang around a bit. What, do you, like, only wait tables while the band's on?"

She just shrugged as she stood up, smiling to herself as she made her way onstage. Once behind the drums, tapping lightly to warm up, she looked back at her.

Teesha was staring at her as if she was an alien from another planet. She pointed at her and mouthed, 'You?', then circled a finger at the rest of the band, 'with them?'

Codi smiled and nodded, the set began, and she lost herself in heartbeats and even managed to forget that Teesha was there, until the last slow song of the night, when she saw the crow girl on the dance floor – with Enrique of all people.

Codi felt a pang of jealousy, even though there was nothing between her and the handsome barman. Still, she was grateful to note that it was obviously a polite dance, for their bodies were nowhere near touching. Codi thought Teesha was luckier than she knew. Carmen was an overly protective mama, and probably weighed twice as much as the athletic black girl.

When the song was over and the band had done their encore

and finally left the stage, Codi walked over to the table where Teesha waited, alone. Enrique had gone back to bartending.

"You brat!" Teesha said immediately, slapping Codi's shoulder in a playful way. "You never told us you were in a band! I wouldna believed it if I hadn't, like, seen it with my own two eyes. You! The shy! The quiet! In a band! Yeah for You!"

Codi was enjoying the other girl's amazement. She was surprised that, for once, having someone be impressed with her for being in a band felt good. When guys had started behaving far more friendly to her at the club than they did anywhere else, she hadn't trusted it, especially with the warning the band members had given her.

She figured they must be drunk or thought every 'musician' was sexy. She didn't know what they wanted, but to a girl who was used to being invisible, particularly invisible to men, their attentions had always seemed false.

Teesha's, on the other hand, felt wonderful. "Thanks a lot," she said. "I know I was a nothing in high school – not a jock, not a brainer, and certainly not cool – but that doesn't mean I really am a nothing."

"Never said you were," said Teesha. "Well, like, maybe once or twice," she admitted with her dazzling smile. "But that was before I got to know you ... Has anyone ever told ya that you have the most amazin' golden eyes? You always had a, like, kinda dopey look on your face at school, so I never noticed before."

"Don't go turning into a groupie," Codi teased.

"You wish," Teesha said, smacking her shoulder again.

"Anyway, I noticed that you've already got a boyfriend here," Codi said, tilting her head over at Enrique.

"'Rique? Man, he's too cute! But I also met his mom, and that woman could take me in the first round! No, he was just bein' kind to the girl you'd left, like, sitting alone while you went to play with your friends, ya know?"

Was Teesha warming up? Codi couldn't believe it. At the end of a week with more stress than she'd felt her whole life, here she was having more fun than she could remember. She felt a moment's guilt, thinking of the missing kids, then told herself not only was she not to blame for their problems, but that she was doing all she could to help.

"Last call," Enrique shouted over to them, and when Codi nodded, he brought colas to the table. But instead of heading back to the bar, the handsome Latino sat down with them, shuffling his chair closer to Codi as if to give a message to Teesha. Codi was baffled. What was going on?

"Another friend I didn't know you had, Codi?" he asked, smiling. "You are definitely a woman of mystery."

Woman? Codi had never thought of herself this way, and it was an uncomfortable thought. On top of that, she couldn't very well tell him that Teesha wasn't actually her friend, particularly since it seemed she seemed to be turning into one. She also felt acutely nervous to be sitting this close to him. She must smell like a wet goat after sweating so hard all night!

If he noticed, he didn't say a word. In fact, he slung a long arm across the backrest of Codi's chair in a proprietary way that amazed her. The problem was, they couldn't exactly speak about anything that was going on in front of this human. It was awkward, and after a few minutes of meaningless small talk, Enrique seemed to take the hint and excused himself to go shut down his cash.

"We should be going," Codi said after they drank their sodas in silence for a minute after he left. "They'll be locking up."

"He your boyfriend?" Teesha asked finally, her eyebrows up near her hairline.

"What? Enrique? You kidding?"

"I saw the way you looked at him, and I saw the way he looked at you. If he's not your boyfriend, you're an idiot," said Teesha with her usual lack of tact.

"Thanks," said Codi sarcastically. "I'm pretty sure he doesn't look at me 'that way' at all."

"Yeah, right. You keep thinking that … What's your problem? You gay?"

"What? No, I'm not gay. I'm just … not ready to date," said Codi defensively. She had always thought this was true … until now.

"Okay, okay, none of my business. Sorry I asked. It just looked like there was something between you, and you know how nosy I am," laughed Teesha. "I'll drive ya home if ya want," the crow Shifter offered in apology.

"Thanks, but I live walking distance from here."

"Okay, but actually, I was, like, thinking I'd leave my car 'n purse 'n stuff at your place and fly home from there, if that's okay. That way, when I show up with where the missing kids are, we'll be able to, like, take off in the car to go rescue 'em."

"I thought crows couldn't fly at night."

"Yeah, way out in the country, not. But here in the city there's, like, always light. No problemo. So, how 'bout it?"

The idea of Teesha seeing how poor she really was made Codi want to say no, but that shouldn't matter, so she quickly agreed and added, "Can you hang on a sec? I've got to go collect my pay."

"Always time f'money, girl."

Codi jumped up and went over to get her thin wad of bills from Frank, who paid them in cash at the end of each night, in what was apparently a long-standing tradition among musicians. From what she understood, not only could you not necessarily count on being invited back the next night, but musicians sometimes had other fish to fry, and wanted to take their money and run. This summer she was making two hundred dollars a night, which added up to living wages for two nights' work. Even her father was impressed.

She stuck the money in a pocket and returned to see Enrique and Carmen saying goodbye to Teesha. She realized they probably thought Teesha was her friend and were being extra nice to her. How could she explain having someone like Teesha for a friend? Then she heard the judgment in her thoughts, and was ashamed. She had always dismissed T-Squared as shallow, vain rich girls, but that wasn't what she was seeing now, at all.

Somehow, becoming something like actual friends with Teesha had made Codi tongue-tied, and she couldn't think of anything to say as they drove home. Teesha chattered about everything and nothing, seeming a little nervous herself. There was a moment's awkward silence as she pulled the car to a stop in front of the Gardiner's house.

"So, I guess I'll see you around?" Codi said as they stood together beside the car, sounding lame even to herself. She had never actually cared what anyone thought of her before. It was a weird feeling. "So ... um ... you're going to shift here, and then, um, fly off?"

"Yeah, that's sorta the plan," said Teesha.

She turned to lead the other girl around to the back of the house, but before she could take a step, there was a hand on her arm stopping her. As she turned, Teesha drew her into a hug. "I'll be seein' ya real soon, Code," she said, sounding as uncomfortable as Codi felt. "And I'm not gonna tell Tosh what you do at that club. Let her, like, find out for herself one a these days, when this mess is all behind us."

"I can hardly wait," laughed Codi, and she led the other girl around the house and down the steps to her back door.

Teesha placed her keys in her purse and handed it to Codi.

"Um ..." she began, obviously embarrassed again. "So ... If you would be so kind as to turn your back, I'll just shift and be off ... Could you keep my stuff somewhere handy, so it'll, like, be ready if I return in a hurry?"

"Sure ... 'Bye," Codi said, turning her back. She heard a flutter of wings, turned in time to see the crow fly over her head, and she was gone.

After a quick shower, Codi shifted into coyote, and spent much of the rest of the night staring at the moon through an open window, wanting to howl with the kind of loneliness she'd heard from other coyotes, but had never really understood until now.

Chapter Five:

Bam! Bam! Bam! They were shooting at her, and she was running. Bam! Bam! Bam! ... Bam! Bam! Bam! What did they have, machine guns?

Codi opened her eyes, her heart pounding, and looked around in panic. Oh. A dream. Then she heard it again. Bam! Bam! Bam! Someone was pounding at the door. She glanced at the clock. Seven-twenty in the morning. Great. She must have had all of five hours' sleep.

Bam! Bam! Bam! "Hang on, hang on," she said to no one in particular as she dragged herself out of bed, feeling groggy and stupid. She slouched over to the door and opened it, just as a petite dark fist was about to strike it again.

"Shhhh," Codi whispered as she opened the door wider to allow the crow girls to enter. "My landlords are – I mean were, I'm sure – trying to sleep. Excuse me for just one minute," she said over her shoulder as she retreated to the bedroom to pull on jeans and a clean t-shirt.

"Now, is there some reason for this early-bird visit?" Codi said, re-entering the tiny kitchen. She felt more awake now, though she went straight to plug in the kettle for coffee.

"Some of us didn't get much sleep last night." She slumped onto one of the two stools standing beside the counter.

"Sorry, Code, but this is an emergency," said Tosha, unplugging the kettle while Teesha handed her her shoes. "Put these on. There's no time to waste."

She was too tired to argue, so she did as she was told, and a moment later was being dragged out the door. She was shoved unceremoniously into the back of their waiting car, where an irresistible odor awaited.

She looked down. A large brown bag with a Micky D's symbol on it sat on the floor of the car. She hesitated, thinking the idea of food was too good to be true.

"Go ahead," Tosha said as she rammed the car into first gear and jerked out around the other parked cars.

"Yeah, we already ate, that's yours," said Teesha from the passenger's side. "We just took a wild guess at what you'd like, so don't get mad, okay?"

Codi dove into the bag. Three egg mcmuffins! Hallelujah! And a large coffee, which she immediately picked up. "I don't suppose ..." she began, but Teesha was already leaning over the backrest and dropping a handful of sugar packets into her lap, along with a stir stick and a couple of creamers.

"I take back every bad thing I've ever said about you two," Codi said. "You're angels, that's what you are. Angels of mercy."

"What bad things?" asked Tosha, but Teesha shoved her on the shoulder and told her to shush, couldn't she see the girl needed to be eating and not talking?

Codi picked up all six sugars, lined them up, shook them, tore the tops three quarters of the way off all six, and dumped them simultaneously into the cup, held precariously between her knees.

"I think you've done this before," Teesha teased her, watching the procedure with undisguised amusement from the front seat.

Codi nodded silently because she was busy stirring, adding cream, re-sealing the lid, opening the flap, and drinking a long hot sip. "Ahhhhh," she said. "Cawwww-feeee."

She reached down into the bag and brought up the first mcmuffin, unwrapping it and wolfing it down in three bites. The other two followed quickly, interspersed with liberal doses of coffee.

When she had let out a final, satisfied belch and excused herself, Teesha said with obvious disgust, "Well, I'd say that was all coyote if I hadn't seen three guys do the same thing while we were waiting for our order. Do you people even bother to taste what you eat?"

"Food ... good," Codi said in a caveman voice. She was feeling much better. "Okay, I'm fully conscious now. What's going on? Something to do with the missing kids?"

"We wish," said Tosha from the driver's seat. "It's Pook. It looks like her gang is revving up for a battle with a rival gang."

"At this hour?" Codi asked incredulously. "I thought gang members didn't even wake up until sometime in the evening."

"Who said they'd been to sleep?" said Teesha. "Nope, they've been drinking and toking and who knows what else all night, far as we can tell. We just went there maybe an hour ago to check on the wee Pookster."

"Yeah, Codi, you're not the only one worried about those missing kids. We've been plenty busy checking that out too," said Tosha.

Codi noticed that both girls had dropped their annoying valleygirl accents, but decided not to mention it.

She was almost beyond gratitude, and quite touched, that it had occurred to them to get her some food, even if it was mctrashies.

The long chase the day before, plus maybe some leftover drug from the hunter's dart, had made her feel sick when they got her out of bed. Now she felt almost normal again.

"Sorry, I never meant to imply you weren't worried about the Shifter kids," she said, "Unless you've also found out where they are?"

"Nothing that lucky," said Teesha.

"Can we discuss that later?" said Tosha, pulling the car over to the curb. "We're here."

Silently, the three Shifters got out of the car, and the two girls led Codi down eight blocks to a rusted metal fire escape running up the side of a six-story building. They climbed to the top, Codi panting heavily, then she followed them across the building. When they got near the far edge, both girls dropped to their knees and crawled forward.

It was a good thing, Codi decided, given the rough surface of the roof, that the girls had opted for track suits in lieu of their usual getups, because her knees hurt right through her jeans when she got down too, and came up alongside Teesha. They lay down and peered gingerly over the side.

Far below, the two gangs faced off on a deserted street. The sun was not yet above the taller buildings, and the scene below was still in semi-darkness. It looked like something from West Side Story, thought Codi, except these guys had real guns and knives and were probably stupid enough to use them. She couldn't see Pook in either group, and gently tapped Teesha on the shoulder, raising her eyebrows and shoulders to indicate her confusion.

Teesha pointed. At the back of the left-hand group, the three girls from the gang were sitting on the curb, smoking something that probably wasn't a cigarette, and carefully not looking at the standoff.

Codi and the crow girls were too high up to hear the exact words, but it was obvious the gangs were yelling insults and threats at one another. Codi couldn't help smiling as she thought about all the nature shows she'd watched where males of the species made threatening noises more often than they actually fought.

She forced her mind back to the present, deciding she must need more sleep if she was finding this funny. Someone could die down there any second. She was actually surprised it hadn't happened already. What were they waiting for?

She was thinking about heading back down to ground level, when she heard a sound behind her, and her stomach clenched with fear. Had someone seen them?

But as she swiveled around to look, Enrique quietly lowered himself beside her. Codi was angry. She gestured, and all four of them backed away from the edge of the roof to converse in whispers.

"What are you doing here?" Codi whispered angrily to Enrique. "Are you stalking me?"

"What? What are You doing here?" Enrique responded, keeping his voice low. "One of the guys down there is probably my cousin. My mom sent me here to make sure he's okay, and I thought I'd check to see if he's even down there before I fling myself into the middle of a gang war."

"Oh." Codi was embarrassed, and a little bit disappointed. It wasn't about her. "So is he?"

"You didn't give me time to check," whispered Enrique, turning and crawling back to the edge to peer cautiously over before crawling back to where they were sitting. "Gracias a Dios, no, he's not there. Now, you didn't tell me why you are here."

"We're friends of a girl down there named Pook," whispered Teesha. "We're worried she's going to get hurt, but we're not sure what we can do to prevent it." She glanced at Codi. "We asked Codi to help us."

"I'll stay, if that's okay," said Enrique. "Maybe I can help, too."

Codi opened her mouth to refuse, thinking that this was Shifter business, but Tosha spoke before she had the chance. "Thanks. You must be Enrique. Teesha told me about you." Tosha's glance at her sister held some unreadable emotion. "We might be able to use your help, so, thanks."

"Good, that's settled," whispered Enrique, and the four of them moved back to the edge of the roof to look down. Enrique lay right beside Codi. She could feel the warmth of his body through his sleeve, and hers. She could feel his even breathing, and found it hard to focus on what was happening below. What was the matter with her?

Finally, after what felt like an hour but was actually just a few minutes of roof gravel biting into her thighs and stomach, something must have snapped. One man – or boy, really, if they were all the same age as the gangers she'd seen the other day – walked forward out of the gang on the right, followed almost immediately by someone from Pook's. The boys circled each other. She couldn't see clearly, but she figured they must be holding knives.

Then, just as the guys began to close on one another, gunshots erupted and bodies began to fall. People were screaming. Enrique and the three Shifters leapt to their feet and ran for the fire escape. Not only were they concerned about Pook, but they didn't want to be trapped when the cops arrived.

When they reached the bottom, it was chaos. From the end of the alley they watched gangers running, hiding in doorways, and firing handguns blindly in the other direction.

Where did kids like these get such weapons? Codi wondered, and then realized, What was I thinking? These kids were never kids. Then she saw a boy no more than eleven or twelve with a bald tattooed head run past laughing. Probably high on something, thought Codi. Guns and drugs were a bad, bad combination.

She looked over at Teesha and Tosha to see what they wanted to do. Her own heart was pounding with fear, but they seemed unreasonably calm. Teesha met her eyes, seemed to read the question in them, and shrugged. Tosha grabbed her arm and pointed.

Halfway down the block across the street, Pook lay on the sidewalk. They couldn't tell whether or not she was alive.

"What are we going to do?" Codi asked. With the guns and the screaming, it was no longer necessary to whisper, but whisper Tosha did, leaning close to Codi so Enrique wouldn't hear.

"Could you shift to coyote and run up there to check her out?" Tosha asked, her tone devoid of teasing for once. At Codi's surprised look, she added, "You make a smaller, faster target."

Codi was about to argue that the girls could shift to crow and fly over there as even smaller, faster targets, when it occurred to her Tosha sounded scared. Really scared. Now she had a real problem, because Enrique was staring at her. He couldn't possibly have heard, but there was no way she was going to shift in front of a human!

Feeling bad, she decided to lie to him again. "I'm going to go for help. You stay here and look out for the girls, okay? Don't want any of us getting shot."

He looked ready to argue, but then shrugged. "Fine."

She turned and ran around the back of the building, where she crouched in the shadows, Shifted to coyote, and then slunk out of the alley into the street, being careful to creep along the very edge of the buildings.

Finally, she had no choice but to cross the street. As she sprang out from the relative safety of the wall, however, she ran directly into the path of three blue dew-ragged gangers who came running around the corner, shooting backwards over their shoulders. Obviously members of the rival gang.

A shot rang out, and one of the boys was hurled back into the other two, who tripped over Codi. The four of them went down in a heap. Codi's back legs were trapped beneath a large body, which wasn't moving. As she struggled to escape, every instinct urged her to snarl and bite the hands and arms of the other two, but it didn't seem wise in the circumstances. A bullet whizzed by close enough to heat one of her ears. It didn't sting, so she hoped she wasn't bleeding, and since two of the boys were still cursing loudly as they tried to untangle themselves, she assumed it had missed them as well.

By the time they were able to get up, and pull the body off of Codi, it was too late for her to get away. For when she looked up, still cringing on her belly, what she saw was the Hispanic leader of the Strykers looming like fat Death, a semi-automatic aimed directly between Codi's golden eyes. Before she could react, though, the boy turned his attention to the gangers Codi had tripped.

Codi expected a quick and bloody exchange, but she was wrong.

"Lose the guns, dawgs," the Stryker leader said quietly, despite the cacophony of gunfire and shouting all around them. Codi thought he sounded more tired than angry. Maybe gang wars weren't all that much fun for him, either.

For a moment, the rival ganger boys looked like they would shoot it out at close range after all, and Codi thought she was done for. Then they slowly put their guns on the ground and slid them away.

"Smart," he said. "Now git outa here ... An' take yo' damn dawg wit' you."

Faster than Codi would have believed, the boys were running away. Codi followed, her tail tucked between her legs. She didn't bother to look back to see if the fat kid was watching, but when the opportunity presented itself, she ducked into an alley and circled back behind the buildings until she was again near Pook.

Codi looked carefully both ways before emerging this time, and a second later was beside the unconscious girl, whom she quickly realized was bleeding from a leg wound. She licked Pook's face, trying to wake her up and get her off the street, but the rabbit girl wouldn't come around. It seemed there was nothing to do but report to Teesha and Tosha, so she dashed down the sidewalk and crossed the street like a golden blur to shift behind the building and then enter the alley where the girls and Enrique were hiding.

"I tried to make the call but my cell phone's dead. So then I went to have a look at Pook. She's bleeding, and she doesn't look like she's going to wake up," she told them.

"We've got to get her out of there," said Enrique and Tosha at the same time.

"Right," said Teesha. "Let's go."

There was no way it was any safer for four young people than it had been for one coyote to rush out into the street in the middle of a gun battle, but that's just what they did.

There were people running in both directions, but no one seemed to pay them the least attention as they inched along the side of the buildings, hoping to avoid flying bullets. In the echoing concrete canyon, every gunshot sounded like it was right behind them, and Codi couldn't help being jumpy.

Wow, she thought. I spend my whole life in peace and calm,

and in the last week I've been shot at twice. This summer isn't exactly going the way I planned.

Before they could reach Pook, a girl who might have been the goth girl from the gang – although in this environment, she probably had dozens of clones – banged into Codi as she raced away from the gunfight.

"Sorry," Codi said reflexively, although it was the girl who'd hit her.

The girl turned her head to say over her shoulder as she kept running, "You got any brains, dorks, you'll get outa here b'fore you get yourselves killed." And she was gone, darting into an alley further ahead. It was good advice, thought Codi. Too bad we can't take it.

Then they were at Pook's side, and without saying a word, Enrique lifted Pook by the shoulders and Codi and Teesha lifted the unconscious girl's legs while Tosha watched for danger. They carried the rabbit girl as quickly as they could into the nearest alley. Fresh gunfire erupted just as they were turning, shattering a brick only a few inches from Codi's face.

She nearly dropped the girl as a shard ripped into in her right shoulder, but she held on. A moment later they were able to put Pook down behind a dumpster. Codi sank to the ground and leaned against the wall, feeling dizzy. She could feel blood trickling down her arm.

"Let me see!" said Enrique. There was no need to keep his voice down, because the gunfire and screaming in the street drowned out any noise they might make.

"Forget it," said Codi, pushing him away. "Just a flesh wound," she added, with a tight smile. She got serious again when she saw Tosha bending over Pook's chest.

Enrique was looking at the rabbit girl, too, with horror in his eyes. "Is she ...?"

"Alive," said Tosha. "But we gotta wake her up."

She lifted the girl's shoulders and said, "Pook, Pook, come on baby, come back to us." When this had no result, she slapped the girl's cheek, hard.

"Uh ..." said Pook, her eyelids fluttering open. "Where ... Who ...?"

"We're friends," said Tosha. "Like you. Come on, girl, you've got to Shift and get rid of that boo-boo down there."

Codi couldn't believe the crow girls were going to make Pook Shift in front of a human. It was forbidden to reveal their secret! But what choice was there? She had to distract him.

"Enrique, could you come look at my shoulder, please?"

"Changed your mind?" He looked glad of the excuse to look away from Pook but also confused. Maybe he had heard the word Shift but didn't understand or believe what he was hearing. He came and squatted beside Codi with his back to the other girls. He helped her remove her jacket and then gently pulled back the sleeve of her T-shirt to reveal a long gouge which was oozing blood. Codi looked away. She had never been particularly good with blood but decided it would be most inconvenient to faint. She glanced back.

Enrique was taking off his bandanna and wrapping it gently around her arm as a bandage. She could feel his breath on her bare skin. He smelled good, too. Whether from shock or some other feeling she couldn't identify, Codi began to shiver.

He quickly reached down and picked up her jacket to drape over her shoulder. She couldn't tell him how easily she could rid herself of the wound by Shifting to coyote and back, so she let him continue to treat her injury and turned her attention back to the rabbit girl.

Pook's eyes had followed Tosha's pointing finger down to the oozing wound on her thigh.

For a moment, it looked like she was going to faint again, but Tosha shook her, harder than Codi thought necessary.

"Stay alert girl, come on," Tosha said roughly. She seemed oblivious to the fact that there was a human only a couple of yards away who was about to find out what they really were. Codi saw fear in Pook's eyes as the rabbit girl struggled to pull herself out of Tosha's grasp. "That's it," encouraged Tosha, "I knew you had some fight in you ... now Shift, dammit, and fix that leg!" Tosha turned to Teesha. "Look away, sis, the girl needs a little privacy. Why don't you go make sure no one tries to join our little party?"

She nodded toward the alley entrance, and as Teesha got up and crept back toward the street, which had become strangely silent. In the eerie quiet, Codi heard some low moaning and some more harsh words from the crow girl to Pook.

Suddenly she understood what Tosha had been doing. She was engaging Pook's fight-or-flight reflexes. Rabbits would choose flight over fight every time, but when cornered could be nasty fighters. If Pook couldn't run, the only way to get her to act was a fight. It was a good strategy, and Codi hoped it worked. She was amazed, and impressed, by the crow girls' calm and toughness. Maybe their lives hadn't been as cushy as she'd imagined.

A minute later Teesha returned from the street and said the gunfight appeared to be over. Codi was surprised to hear no sirens – no police and no ambulances. Surely one of these kids had a cell phone? – Or didn't gangers call 911? She wasn't sure how far the nearest active business was – this whole district seemed abandoned – so maybe no one had notified the authorities yet.

Just as Enrique was sitting back after draping Codi's jacket on her, there was a hand on her good arm. "Code, girl, it's your turn," said Teesha, not even looking at the handsome Latino.

"What about Pook?"

"She's okay. She Shifted and then Shifted back, leaving the injured tissue. It's a bit gross looking, but no worse than the kind of pizza Tosha likes." She looked directly at Enrique, and then back at Codi, as if daring her to tell him the truth about what she was.

It was confusing. Codi's parents had told her over and over again that if any human found out what they really were, they would have to run away and never come back. Codi liked her life here. She liked their apartment. She liked drumming with the band. Why was Teesha trying to ruin it for her? Codi felt sick to her stomach.

Codi tried to avoid the problem by asking, "So what's Pook doing now?"

"Tosha's talking to her ... I don't think that part is going so well."

Codi could hear the argument and looked over in time to see Pook jerk her arm out of Tosha's grip.

"Back off! Who do you think you are, my mother?" Then Pook noticed Enrique, Codi and Teesha. "What's this, the cavalry? You guys the friggin' Red Cross? Nobody asked for your help! I've gotten along just fine without you up till now, and I'll be fine long after you've gone back under whatever rock you crawled out from."

Codi didn't know the rabbit girl. She hadn't gone to the same school. Still, the tough words sounded strange coming out of such a baby face.

Pook had stood and was trying to get past them. Codi wasn't in much shape for wrestling with an angry teen, even if the girl was barely five feet tall. Nevertheless, she and Teesha moved to block Pook's path, glancing over at Tosha for direction.

"Let her go." The beautiful young woman sounded suddenly old. "She's right. We're not her parents, all we did was save her friggin' life. There's nothing we can do to stop her from throwing it away again."

If Pook was affected by these angry words, she gave no sign. Codi was just glad the girl was walking without a limp. She wondered for a moment if anyone had seen Pook get shot. If so, they were going to be pretty surprised to see an uninjured girl coming back.

On the other hand, so much had been happening, she could see how easy it would be to doubt your own eyes, to believe you hadn't seen what you'd thought you'd seen in the middle of something as horrifying as the battle they'd just witnessed.

After Pook had stalked out of the alley and disappeared down the street, it was Codi's turn to shift. She didn't want Enrique trying to take her to a hospital, and she didn't think he would accept her statement that she didn't need a doctor. This was it. She'd have to tell him the truth and then never see him again. Her parents had warned her that this moment comes to all Shifters – she would have to walk away.

But she wasn't ready. She wasn't ready for a boyfriend, and she sure wasn't ready for a human boyfriend! But she discovered she also wasn't ready to leave behind her life with the band, and whatever it was she had with the handsome Latino.

Teesha came to her rescue. "Our car's parked not far from here," she said to Enrique. "Tosh and I will drive Codi to the hospital. Thanks for all your help." She was holding out her hand.

Enrique seemed ready to argue, but when he looked over at Codi, she dropped her eyes, and he took the hint.

"All right, then, I guess everything here is okay, so I'll just head back to the bar," he said. "I'll tell the band you can't work for a week or two, okay?"

Codi wanted to argue, wanted to say that she'd be good as new in about five minutes, but she had to maintain the illusion of humanity.

"Oh, sure, thanks. I'll see what the doctor says, and then give Frank a call tomorrow. Thanks again for everything," she finished, putting all of the warmth and gratitude into her voice that her words could not convey.

"What about the gangers? Shouldn't we help them?" he asked.

Tosha answered. "I called 911. The police and ambulances should be here any second. Are you sure you want to try to convince the police that you weren't part of this? We're getting out of here before anyone starts asking us those questions."

"Good point." Enrique turned to Codi held her gaze for a long minute before he came over and gave her a careful hug, then quickly hugged the two crow girls before moving to the entrance to the alley, glancing left and right, and then running across the street and disappearing down another alleyway.

"Okay, girl, saved your bacon there. Now Shift, dammit!"

Codi stepped behind the dumpster while the girls politely waited on the far side. Coming around a minute later, there was no sign of her injury except her torn and bloodied t-shirt, and the inch-long brick fragment she brought to show them.

"Pretty good for a 'flesh wound'," said Teesha.

Tosha examined her shoulder. "It's good. Now let's get the heck out of here before the cops show up or the gangs decide to finish each other off."

They stood for a moment at the mouth of the alley, checking both directions to make sure there were no armed gangers in sight. It was still quiet, which felt strange, especially after the noise and horror of just a few minutes earlier.

"Speaking of cops," said Codi, "shouldn't there have been some around by now?"

"Yeah, maybe in white-bread suburbia," said Tosha.

"In districts like this, where they know nobody hangs out except gangers and winos, the cops don't come unless invited, and maybe not even then," said Teesha.

Codi was grateful things stayed peaceful as they ran to the girls' car. Fortunately, no one had discovered it, so it was still in one piece. They jumped in. Tosha did a quick u-turn and sped out of the area.

It wasn't until they were downtown that Codi began to relax and look out the window. She couldn't help thinking it odd the way people walked so obliviously down the sidewalk, intent on nothing more sinister than a new pair of shoes. Part of her wanted to jump out and shake them, wake them up to the violence and terror that existed a couple of miles, and a world, away.

She shook off the thought. No one had said a word since leaving the alley. They had been too scared and worried to talk. The silence was especially odd from the crow girls, who had always seemed to talk the way most people breathed.

"You guys okay?" she asked from the back seat, finally not able to stand the quiet any longer.

"Yeah, Code, we're fine," said Tosha with a dead voice.

"Oh yeah, we're involved in gang wars all the time, girl," added Teesha sarcastically.

"I've been meaning to ask you about that ... It's none of my business, but I've always assumed you two were from a rich family, from your clothes and this Beamer and all."

"Yeah, Mom's a doctor and Dad's a lawyer, but they grew up in Harlem, and they've made sure we know where that's at," said Tosha.

"Sorry, I didn't mean anything, but when you say things like 'white-bread suburbia' ... I sure didn't grow up there. You're closer to that life than I've ever been."

Teesha looked chastened. "Sorry, Code, I guess it's a reflex. Our parents are always saying things like that, and we forget that not all white people ..."

"Forget it. You two know more about gangs than I do, so I guess I was kind of protected by my parents. Even if it wasn't in 'suburbia'. Sorry if I offended you ... It's just that I was nearly messing myself with fear back there, and you both seemed so calm and brave."

Both girls laughed, and Codi felt better.

"I was terrified, Code," said Tosha. "I almost peed myself."

"Oh yeah," Teesha added with feeling. "Oh, yeah."

"I'm kinda, like, disappointed we weren't able to get Pook outa there, though" said Tosha. "I really thought after what happened to her, ya know ..."

"Yeah, me too," said Teesha. "That little girl don't have the brains her momma gave her, and that's the truth."

Codi found it amusing, petite Teesha calling Pook "little", but she didn't say anything. "I'm sorry, too," she said instead. "I'm glad we were there to maybe save her life, though."

This seemed to cheer the two girls up. Tosha glanced at her watch, and began to laugh. "Can you believe after all that, it's like, only just past nine?"

Codi didn't own a watch, but the position of the sun confirmed that it was still a while before midday. "Wow," she said. "I'm wasn't sure if all that took five minutes or five years."

"I, like, know what you mean, Code," said Teesha.

Codi noticed the girls had resumed their silly accents. She decided this was actually a good thing. They'd been too worried this morning to bother, so this had to mean they were feeling better, even if it bugged her no end. "So, my do-gooding partners, what now?"

"Doncha wanna go home and go back to sleep?" Tosha asked, pulling over to the curb and putting the car in park. She turned to look over the backrest at Codi.

Codi suddenly realized they were on her street. She ought to be exhausted, but she actually felt wired and tense. "Too much adrenaline in the system to sleep just yet. Want to go somewhere and hang out?"

She was surprised to find herself hoping the girls would stay with her a while longer.

Teesha's eyes were shining with warmth as she opened her mouth to speak, but before she could say a word, Tosha said, "Sorry, Code, we've like, gotta go back to see if the Pookster is okay."

"Of course, I understand, good luck, watch out for flying bullets," Codi said quickly, before she started to beg. She felt very small and vulnerable, and she didn't like the feeling.

Life just seemed so pointless and short in the face of the violence they'd just experienced. She didn't want to be alone, but she didn't want them to stay with her out of pity.

"Yeah," Teesha said without enthusiasm, "We'd better go back and make sure she's still alive. Wouldn't want to go to all that work to save her fluffy tail and then have her buy it when we're not looking." She smiled wanly, looking exhausted.

"Maybe I'll see you later, then?" Codi couldn't stop herself from asking.

"What, you like, trying to join our sisterhood, or what?" Tosha asked through the window, laughing as she put the car in gear and lurched out into traffic with her usual driving skill. "Dream on, white girl!"

Codi saw Teesha's hand waving at her out the window as they

drove off. It looked kind of sad. But maybe that was just her imagination.

She paced restlessly for a few minutes, then went into the shadows behind the house and Shifted to coyote. Daylight wasn't her favorite time to be a coyote, especially in the city, but she needed to run around for a bit and burn off some energy. She knew there was a ravine less than a mile away, and she'd be able to blend into the shadows there. No one would see the crazy coyote running like she was being chased by Death.

Chapter Six:

It had felt silly the next day to go to a drug store and waste good money on a sling to wear to visit the band, but Codi thought she didn't have a choice. She had called Frank in the morning, and explained what happened, then promised to come to the club on Friday night to tell them the story. Frank had said he'd be able to find a drummer to work with them temporarily, but had – thank goodness! – made it clear he hoped she be back at work in a couple of weeks. Now it was Friday evening, and she was getting ready to go to the club.

She was irritable and antsy. It bugged her to set around and do nothing. She wanted to just go back to the forest and forget all about the Shifter problems. She hated not being able to drum. It was her favorite escape from stress. She hated having to pretend to be hurt. She hated that who she was, was something she had to keep secret. With a low growl, she was starting to pull on her sneakers, when there was a knock at the door. Not knowing who it might be, she grabbed the sling and pulled it over her head before pulling the door open. Good thing she did, because it was Enrique, with a bouquet of flowers.

"Frank told me where you lived, and that you were coming tonight. I thought you might want a ride over." He held the flowers out sheepishly.

"I don't. Go away." Codi closed the door, refusing to meet his eyes. Why did everyone think they had the right to barge in on her life? A little more than a week ago, she had had her life entirely to herself. And that had suited her just fine. Now it seemed everyone she knew thought they were part of her life! She turned back and sat in her Lazyboy, waiting for him to leave. Strength in solitude! – why did Enrique only now think to find out where she lived?

After a long minute of silence, there was another gentle knock at the door. Sighing, Codi stood and opened it again. "What?"

Enrique was looking down at her bare feet. The flowers had disappeared. "Can I at least help you with your shoes?"

Codi certainly didn't need any help with her shoes. In fact, she didn't usually even tie her shoelaces, but she was tired of fighting, so she just nodded, sitting on a kitchen stool while Enrique struggled to slip each shoe onto her foot and then very carefully tied each shoelace. It was a good thing he was looking down while he worked so that he couldn't see the mischievous grin she couldn't stop from creeping onto her face. The Trickster couldn't help enjoying this. Codi felt a twinge of guilt at letting him work when she was perfectly fine, but it didn't last. What he was doing was no big deal, and she had to maintain her pretense of injury, didn't she?

Also, he was blushing, which made her laugh. Maybe she wasn't the only one a bit awkward around the opposite sex. After he closed the door behind them, he asked her for the key so he could lock it for her. "I'm injured, not brain dead," she told him with her arms crossed across her chest.

"Hey, I just thought it might be hard to turn the key with your arm in a sling," Enrique responded quietly. She wanted to be mad, but realized she couldn't change the game as this point, so she told him her hiding spot, which felt very strange. No one except her parents and the Gardiners knew where the key was hidden. Between them, T-squared, Nadeem, Rashda and now Enrique, her private space wasn't very private any more.

Speak of the devil, Mr. Gardiner arrived on his balcony just as she and Enrique were leaving. "How's the arm?" he called down. She had been wearing the sling whenever she was outside the apartment.

"Getting better already," Codi assured him. "I heal fast. I bet I'll be back drumming by next week."

"Don't rush it," advised the old man. "Don't want to do any permanent damage. – And the missus said to thank your friend for the flowers. They have made her day!"

Codi was quick to pipe up before Enrique spilled the beans about the gang fight and scared the old man into a heart attack. She had told the Gardiners that she had injured her should by drumming too hard. "Oh, so you've already met Enrique? He's the bartender at the club where I play. I'm supposed to go there tonight to see the band, and Enrique very kindly came over to give me a lift, even though he knows there is nothing wrong with my legs." She was glaring at the young man during the last part of her sentence. Then she looked back up at Mr. Gardiner, forcing herself to smile. "But I guess you've met?"

Mr. Gardiner gaze was piercing. "Why, yes. The young man came to our door to tell us that he was picking you up to take you to the bar to visit your band mates, and he gave the flowers to Marie. It was very kind of him to think of us when coming to visit you."

Codi could see the old man suspected what had happened. She didn't get the chance to say anything, however, because Enrique was already responding.

"It was nice to meet you, Mr. Gardiner," Enrique was saying very politely. "I was with Codi when she got injured, so I feel a little bit responsible for making sure she's okay. As for the flowers, that was my pleasure. Please tell your wife that I am always happy to make a beautiful woman smile." He looked pointedly at Codi. "Now this one — she isn't smiling at all today. I know her arm is hurt, but I have been as chivalrous as I can be, and still, no smile."

Codi turned to him and pasted as false a smile on her face as she could manage. "Happy?" she said through gritted teeth. What, did he think the Gardiners were her parents? Was he trying to cause trouble for her? But when she looked in his eyes, she saw definite mischief there.

Luckily, Mr. Gardiner had missed the hint. "Good, good," he was saying. "It's nice to see someone taking care of Codi for a change. She's a bit too independent, if you ask me."

This was the first Codi had heard that Mr. Gardiner thought she was too independent. What was next? Was she turning into a Disney princess waiting for a Prince Charming? Ugh!!

"Well, we should be going," said Enrique smoothly, ducking back under the balcony to hide the key in its usual spot. "The band will be waiting to see Codi."

"Of course! Have a good time!" said Mr. Gardiner, beaming. "Glad to see Codi getting out of the apartment. It isn't like her to be such a homebody."

On the street in front of the building sat Enrique's car, an aging Chev that looked like the second cousin of Codi's ancient motorcycle. The handsome Latino swung open the passenger door for her with a gallant sweep of his arm, then quickly closed it and locked it when Codi walked straight past him, heading down the sidewalk toward the club.

"It would be faster to drive," he called, racing to catching up with her.

She turned to look at him for a long moment and then deliberately turned away and kept walking. At the moment, she was finding it hard to remember why she had liked him.

"Why don't you take your car and go? I'm perfectly capable of walking to the club myself!"

"Hey!" he said, pocketing his car keys and continuing to walk beside her. "You're independent. I get that. I thought I was your friend, but I guess I'm nobody to you. I get that, too. I'm just trying to be nice. What's that, a crime around you?"

She felt a twinge of guilt when she heard him say he was nobody to her. If he had shown such interest in her before all of this started, before it appeared that she was helpless, she might have been very interested in him! She just didn't like it that he only seemed to take a real interest in her once he thought she needed help. Was he actually into her, or just playing Mr. White Knight? There would be no way to tell, now. Her shoulders slumped. She gave herself a shake. There was no future in a relationship with a human, anyway, she reminded herself grumpily.

Enrique was uncharacteristically silent for the rest of the way to the club. When they got there, he held the door open for her and followed her in, but didn't even turn to say a word before heading behind the bar to start work. Codi felt hurt, then chided herself for the feeling. You were rude to him, so he was rude to you, she told herself. So what?

A moment later she was surrounded by her bandmates, and the bad feelings about Enrique faded as she told the 'safe' version of the story about the gang battle – leaving out the Shifting parts, of course

. She assured them that she was almost better, and that she'd be back drumming the following weekend. It bugged her even more that she had to pretend to be injured instead of working.

It bugged her worse that she had to listen to another drummer playing her drums! She hadn't realized how attached she had become to the band, and her part in it.

She could hear her dad's voice in her mind. "Shifters don't get attached to humans. You're just going to have to move on in the end, so it's best if you don't get started."

She'd always known better than to argue with him, but in this case hadn't even wanted to because she considered herself a loner who did what she wanted to do when she wanted to do it, and had always felt proud of her self-containment.

Tonight, she was left feeling distinctly lonely as she watched the band perform. She could have gotten up and joined the crowd on the dance floor, but her heart wasn't in it. She was sitting, running an absent finger around and around the rim of her glass of soda, when a shadow blocked the light and she turned to see Enrique seating himself in an empty chair at her table.

"You looked a bit lonely," he said, unnerving her. "I came over to see if you want to dance."

"Stop rescuing me!" she replied, more irritably than she felt. "You are not my white knight, and I don't need your sympathy!"

"Settle down, Chiquita!" He was smiling as if she hadn't just barked at him. "I thought I was your friend! Can't a friend ask a friend to dance?"

She opened her mouth to say something sarcastic, but as she glanced at his face, she could suddenly see his vulnerability in the hesitant quirk of his smile. Her tough attitude melted. He really was such a sweet guy!

When the next song started, it was a salsa, her favorite. She had taught herself the steps from videos on YouTube but had always felt too shy to try the Latin dance in front of Latinos. Besides, she was always playing when this song was on. It was too great a temptation to pass up. So she stood up and offered him her good hand, leaving the other in the sling. Enrique leapt to his feet like a happy Labrador, and she couldn't help smiling at his eagerness.

On the dance floor, the first few moments were awkward as Enrique figured out how to hold her by her 'good' hand, and as they got their feet in time to each other as well as the music. But more quickly than she could have imagined, she was actually dancing the dance she had practiced so many hours in her basement apartment!

Enrique was smiling ear to ear, too, and her heart stretched with happiness. It helped that he was such a good dancer. He recovered smoothly when they faltered in moving together or apart. It helped when she forgot herself completely and let the music take over as she always did when drumming.

Codi found she was actually sorry when the song ended a few short minutes later. She turned to head back to the table, but stopped when Enrique tugged on her good hand. "Not so fast, Belleza. Are you tired already? I didn't think your feet had been injured."

Had he really just called her Beautiful? She didn't know what to think. Her parents weren't that affectionate and no one had ever called her pretty in her life. As she'd been taught to do, she had worked hard at being invisible, so she hadn't really thought about it.

She was surprised how hot her face felt as she blushed with pleasure at the compliment.

He was already moving to the music of the next song, and before she could change her mind, she allowed herself the pleasure of dancing with a handsome guy. This song was meringue, and she had never looked up the dance moves for this kind of dance, but the rhythm was in her blood and it was only seconds before she and Enrique were moving smoothly together.

As the song slowed to the end, though, Enrique pulled her against him, circling her small waist with his arm and burying his face in her hair. Codi could see other couples doing the same thing, but it was too much for her. She pushed him away, turned, and ran out of the bar, feeling tears running down her cheeks as she ignored his shouts of, "I'm sorry! Come back!"

She kept running, all the way home. She was scared, and ashamed. Part of her brain knew that Enrique hadn't really done anything wrong, nor had she, but she felt that she had crossed a line; a line she was not ready to cross.

When she reached the apartment, she slowed down so she could enter as silently as possible in order not to wake the Gardiners. As she slipped into her bed a few minutes later, she didn't allow her mind to dwell on the happiness she'd felt dancing with the handsome Latino. She told herself that that was a life that would never be hers. Best not to wish for something you will never have. She felt that she should Shift to coyote again and go out hunting mice to remind herself of what she really was, but for once, she didn't want to be an animal. She wished with all her heart that she was just what Enrique thought she was – a human girl. Sleep was a long time coming.

Chapter Seven:

"Code! Code! Open up!"

She woke up, disoriented, not knowing where she was.

"Code!"

Forcing herself to her feet, she stumbled to the door still not knowing what time, or even what day it was. She yanked the door open, and Teesha burst into the room.

"I found them! I know where they are. Come on, girl! Get your shoes on! There's no time to lose. Where's my purse?"

Codi flopped down onto the floor to pull her sneakers on over her bare feet, still groggy and dazed. Why did the crows always do this to her?

Teesha had found her purse herself, and was pulling on Codi's arm before her second foot was all the way into the shoe. "Wake up, sleepyhead. It's four in the afternoon! This is it!"

"Where?" she managed to ask as she slumped into the front seat beside the crow girl. "How?"

"The truck came to the parking lot about an hour ago," Teesha explained as she pulled a terrifying u-turn in traffic and tore off down the street. Codi held her breath, but they miraculously managed not to get hit. "Rashda was doing the garbage can thing, and Tosh and I were watching from a tall pine tree."

"Rashda? Not Nadeem?"

"Apparently, they agreed to take turns. Now she's been taken!"

"So what'd she do, run out in front of them?"

"Rashda's not that stupid, Code. She waited until they saw her and took off – at a raccoon's gallop, can you believe it? – and of course, they went running after her – and I don't even think she was faking how scared she was."

"Poor Rashda."

"Yeah, well, there wasn't even time to chicken out ... So anyways, she was making a lot of noise, so they, like, had no trouble tracking her, and them BAM! We heard the shot from where we were following, flying just over the treetops. I was almost too scared to go down and look, but Tosh shot down through the trees like a rocket, you know? So I had to follow and when we got to the spot, one of those rednecks had poor unconscious Rash picked up by the tail and was stuffing her into a canvas sack. Good thing we're so dark or they have caught us, too, sitting there on a tree branch no more than a hundred yards away."

The crow girl had hardly paused for breath during this entire explanation, and had been simultaneously lurching the car from lane to lane as she fought through downtown traffic. Teesha had the nasty habit of speeding toward the car in front of her, then slamming on the brakes at the last second, just as Codi was sure they were about to rear-end someone. She had given up watching, preferring to die with her eyes closed. On top of that, she was finding it impossible to follow the story, even with her eyes shut. However, if there had been more to it she'd never know, because Teesha suddenly swooped the car to a stop and jumped out without a word.

When Codi opened her eyes she was surprised to see they were on the other side of town, way out on the Strip, where fast-food joints, strip malls, and seedy motels lined both sides of the highway. They were parked along the far edge of an obviously abandoned strip mall.

She climbed warily out of the car, but before she could open her mouth, Teesha put her fingers to her lips then took her hand and led her down a narrow alley between one strip mall and the next. As they emerged behind the plaza, Codi could see the place that was, most likely, their destination.

A squat, ugly, cement-block building stood at the other end of a parking lot overgrown with small trees and weeds which had pushed their way up through the pavement. Even with the new growth, there still wouldn't be much cover to approach the building, so Codi turned to Teesha, the question on her lips.

Teesha was one step ahead of her, backing silently into the alleyway, and turning her back. In the shadows of the narrow space, Codi saw her shift into crow. A moment later, the small black bird was lifting into the air, nodding its head at her and landing on the roof. Quickly, Codi stepped into the alley, shifted, and a moment later was creeping almost invisibly in coyote form through the scattered undergrowth of the lot.

Just as she was nearing the building, there was a shout from behind it. Crawling on her belly, she circled around until she could see what was going on. A black bird was attacking a man who stood on a ramp leading down to delivery doors in the basement. Tosha! She was swooping and pecking and darting away before the man could grab her. Why hadn't she waited for them?

Codi dashed forward and snapped at the man's leg, getting a mouthful of dirty jeans. Then another black bird joined the attack. Teesha! The man was protecting his head with his arms, and cursing loudly. What did they think they were doing? What if the other hunters were nearby? Sure enough, the rogue Shifter emerged from the open delivery doors a moment later, gun in hand.

Codi turned and began to run. The rogue looked back inside over his shoulder, shouted, "Close this door and get out here!" into the building, and raised the gun to his shoulder. However, he was aiming at the birds still harassing the other hunter rather than at Codi, so Codi stopped and barked at him, distracting him and at the same time trying to warn the crow girls to fly away. The rogue swung his rifle toward Codi, but instead of retreating, one of the birds attacked the Shifter, cawing angrily. Damn it! This wasn't how it was supposed to go! Codi retreated backward and to the right, becoming nearly invisible in the undergrowth.

Then she heard a shot, and looked up in time to see a bird plummet to the ground, black feathers floating gently after. Teesha? Her heart sank, but she didn't dare move. If she got shot too, it wouldn't help anyone. A shadow crossed over her head as the other bird flew away. She heard another shot and looked up in time to see the bird twist, dive, and thankfully keep going. As she began to back slowly away, Codi heard the rogue Shifter's ugly voice say, "Peek it up and put it een a cage! Queek, before we are attacked again!"

Codi retreated to the shadows of the alley, and shifted in time to be grabbed by Teesha. "Tosha!" the crow girl was sobbing quietly.

"They've got Tosha!"

Codi held the other girl for a moment in silence, stroking her braided hair and letting her cry.

"What are we gonna do, Code?" Teesha whispered finally, pulling away.

"I don't know, Teesh. Do you know why she was attacking that guy?"

"We didn't exactly have time for a conversation."

"Sorry, I just can't believe she thought she could take them on herself."

"Tosh thinks with her heart, not her head," said Teesha, tears still rolling down her cheeks which she didn't even bother to brush away. "What are we gonna do?"

"Well, first we need to check things out, find out exactly where they're holding her and the other kids. Then we'll figure out a way to rescue them all." Codi spoke with more confidence than she felt, but it must have been okay, because after a moment, Teesha's crying slowed, and then stopped.

"Okay," she said, sniffing. "You're right. Standing here ain't fixin' nothing."

They shifted again, and once more headed across the lot. As Codi neared the building, a shadow crossed her head, and she ducked down in fear. Then she looked up and saw that it was Teesha landing on the roof. Ignoring the crow, she crept forward until she could peer through the thick weeds, unseen, into a basement window. Surprisingly, the room was almost empty, although there were dozens of empty cages stacked against the far wall.

Then she noticed two raccoons huddled in cages barely bigger than they were. These could only be Rashda and some other poor

Shifter, and the cardinal – Ariana? – was in a tiny cage looking bedraggled and tired, her eyes closed. She needed to see if there was any way into the room. The window she'd been peering through was glass with metal bars. It looked like it was locked solid.

Two men came into view, obviously the hunters from the forest, rifles slung from their shoulders. The rogue Shifter was saying, "I weel be happy when we collect enough aneemals and can deleever them to Señor Drogas in Colombia. Tell that other bum Yake een there to stop stuffing heez face, an' make certain each aneemal gets el agua – how you say – water. They muz stay healthy. Theez leetle aneemals are going to make us all reech." He laughed without humor, and Codi shivered despite the heat.

The coyote girl slowly backed away from the window. Breaking in or out wasn't going to be easy. She had noticed that one corner of the window was missing. However, the gap was only an inch or two wide, so Codi couldn't see how it helped. She turned and slunk along the wall to the front of the building. It was too exposed to check out, but had to be the main entrance. The pickup truck was missing, so the hunters had probably driven it inside the delivery entrance in the back. It was no doubt parked somewhere inside. Damn! So much for sabotaging the truck!

As she came back around the corner of the building, she almost knocked Teesha off her feet. The crow girl was looking into the basement and was obviously extremely upset. She pecked at Codi's leg, and tilted her head back at the window. Codi looked in again. On a table over to the right was another small cage – this one holding a black bird who was hopping up and down and throwing itself uselessly against the woven wire walls.

Tosha! On the far side of the table, the third hunter was stuffing a submarine sandwich into his large mouth while mustard dripped unnoticed onto his pants. His rifle lay beside the cage.

Codi wished desperately that she could say something to Teesha, or at least hug her again, but their current forms denied her both these things, so she did as any coyote would do to comfort another of its kind – she licked along the side of the bird's face. She couldn't tell if Teesha appreciated or resented this gesture because she gave no sign, turning away to fly back up to the roof.

There was nothing she could do for Teesha or her cousin at the moment anyway. She retraced her route, crossing the abandoned parking lot and shifting back into human form.

She didn't see any sign of Teesha, so she figured she must have shifted already. When she got to the car, the other girl was inside crying, her arms and head resting on the steering wheel.

"Hey, there, Teesh, she'll be okay, come on," Codi said as she got in.

Teesha turned an angry, tear-streaked face toward her. "Unless you saw something I didn't, Tosh and the others are trapped down there with those hunters. Barred windows! Locked doors! What are we supposed to do? Knock and ask politely if they will free everyone?"

"I am not your enemy," Codi reminded her quietly.

This seemed to diffuse her anger. "Sorry, Code, I just can't take it … Tosh locked up in a cage! Seriously! What are we gonna do?"

"I honestly don't know, Teesha. I'm not all that great at planning stuff, you know. I'm more of a loner – I usually just do my own thing and let everyone else play leader and follower."

"And I can't think straight. Tosh and I were raised together, we're like sisters. And it makes me nuts to see those Shifter kids locked up like that … Did you find anything out about what's going on?"

Codi explained what she'd heard about Colombia and money,

but said she didn't see what the connection was. "There are lots of cute Shifter kids in South America if it's just kids they want," she said, thinking out loud. "No, that can't be it. There are just as many Shifters in South America as there are here."

They were both silent for a moment. "Maybe ..." they both said at once, then Codi said, "You first."

"Maybe they're afraid that if they took too many local kids, people would get suspicious ... Nah, can't be. All they'd have to do is get them from a few hundred miles away, or some big city down there where kids are abandoned all the time."

"Hey, what about this? If they took local Shifter kids and people found out what they were, they would start to look at each other and wonder who's Shifter and who isn't, wouldn't they? So maybe this rogue Shifter is keeping his own neck safe – how could he explain why he recognizes us and no one else does? And so he wants kids from up here, different enough that he can say we're special, we're unique. That keeps him safe."

"So what do they want American Shifter kids for? Experiments?" Teesha shuddered.

"No, I don't think so. Since when do scientists have enough money to make scumbags rich? No, it's got to be something more mundane ... "

"Like a zoo?" Codi said.

"A zoo?" Teesha said at the same time.

As soon as they said it, they were both nodding.

"Of course! Unique, bizarre. Three shows daily!" Codi said, her face twisted with anger.

"Even if they can't force them to shift, the kids would have to from time to time anyway, and with video surveillance ... Or they could shoot movies! Poor Tosha!"

Teesha looked like she was ready to cry again, so Codi quickly said, "Well, Tosha and the others won't have to worry about that, because we're going to get them out. But we need to know how much time we have before they leave for South America."

"I'll stay here and listen in some more," volunteered Teesha. "You go get help."

"Are you going to be okay?" Codi said as she got out of the car and pulled her bus pass out of the back pocket of her jeans, glad she kept it there but wishing she had brought her motorcycle.

"Not really ... But I'd rather be here keeping an eye on things than worrying what's happening when I'm not watching."

"Good. You watch. Don't do anything. Don't play hero, okay?"

"Of course not. Just hurry back."

"Deal."

They hugged briefly and Teesha hurried down the alley to shift, and Codi crossed the busy road to get to a bus stop. First, Nadeem.

***

"Have you seen Rashda around anywhere?" Nadeem asked the moment he dragged Codi into his and Rashda's apartment. His eyes suddenly grew bright with tears, which surprised Codi. Nadeem was usually the 'stiff upper lip' type.

"Rashda didn't come home last night," he said, his voice quavering. "We've been sharing an apartment this summer while Testing. It was her turn at the park last night. I'm to blame. I should never have agreed to let her be a decoy. She only has one friend, and I've already spoken with her. Taylor hasn't seen Rashda since yesterday. I'm worried sick. I know we aren't supposed to contact our parents, but I'm starting to think we have to! But – ack! – nobody even knows

111

where they are. What I don't know is what to do."

Codi felt her stomach sink as she gathered the courage to tell him what had happened. She quickly filled him in on how Rashda had let herself be captured and how Teesha had taken Codi to the site where the kids were being held. "Rashda is ... locked in a cage like the others, and probably forced to shift by the rogue Shifter, but yeah, she's okay I think."

"The others?"

"Them too." Codi She told Nadeem what she'd heard from the rogue Shifter about the plans for the Shifter kids, and the conclusion she and Teesha had come to. She also told Nadeem about Tosha being captured, ending, "... I figured since you seem to know every Shifter in the city, you'll be able to round up enough help to stage a jail break. But we're going to have to be very careful. We don't want to end up with more Shifters trapped."

"Forget getting help. We're supposed to be adults now, aren't we? And adults solve their problems themselves. Let's go right now and get Rashda and the others out."

"With what?" said Codi gently. "Our bare hands?"

"What we need is a diversion," said Nadeem, sighing. "Maybe when this Shifter jerk isn't around, so the other hunters won't know we're Shifters. If I knew how to make a bomb ..."

"Too dangerous, 'Deem," said Codi. "What if we blew up all the kids instead of rescuing them? ... No, a diversion is a good idea, but it's going to have to be something a little more subtle than a bomb." They were both silent, thinking.

"Okay," Codi said finally, glancing up at a clock that read almost three in the morning. "It's late, and we both have some more thinking to do ... I agree we can't go asking for adult help yet. This is what Testing is all about. Whether we can handle emergencies."

Both Shifters sat silently for a few moments. "Hey! Maybe we can't ask adults, but could you talk to other Shifter kids and find out who might help?"

"I'll have an army gathered to attack first thing in the morning."

"Nadeem, I want to save those kids, too, but I don't think we can just rush in with an army because the hunters have the kids as hostages. Fewer people might be better than more. But. Oh! There are some Shifter teens out in the forest who want to help. I'll get a message to them."

"Okay," said Nadeem, sounding frustrated. "I'll check around town to find out who's with us. Maybe someone will come up with a plan ... Hey! Could we call Animal Control? People aren't allowed to go capturing wild animals and putting them in cages, are they?"

"Good thought, 'Deem, except who knows how long Animal Control would want to hold the kids to make sure they were all right and so on. What if they can't Shift before it's too late? We can't take that chance, same as we can't go to the police ... I'm sorry. I seem to be dumping on your ideas.

"It's okay. You're right, of course." Nadeem sighed, his shoulders slumping. "Tomorrow?"

"Tomorrow," said Codi, shaking her friend's hand before impulsively turning the handshake into a hug. "They're going to be okay, okay?"

"Okay. Thanks, Codi."

Chapter Eight:

It was at dawn a day later that Codi, Teesha, Nadeem, two mice and a snake were huddled whispering in the alley facing the building where the missing kids were being held. Heavy cloud cover made it seem darker than usual, which worked to their advantage, Codi thought. "So, you know what to do?" she said.

"Yep," said Derek, one of the mice, who in human form was actually training to be a jockey.

"Slip through the crack in the window, sneak past those sleeping creeps, and unlock the door," said Deena, the other mouse.

"Let you guys in, we all shift back to human, unlock the cages, and get the heck out of there!" finished Zeke, the snake Shifter.

"Perfect!" said Nadeem, whose plan it was.

"I still don't like it," said Teesha. "I want to be on the inside, getting Tosha out, not sitting outside."

"Someone has to keep watch in case one of the hunters isn't there and shows up while we're opening cages. You know that, Teesha," said Codi.

"Why can't it be you?" said Teesha.

"We've been all through this. I'm going in because if something goes wrong I can use my teeth as a weapon. Nadeem has sharp teeth and claws, too. The others are small enough to get away. You'd just end up sharing a cage with Tosh."

"Yeah, well maybe that'd be better than this," Teesha replied resentfully.

"Teesh ..." Codi said gently.

"Yeah, yeah, get goin'. Time's a wastin'."

"Good girl," Codi said, ignoring the dirty look the crow shot her before she shifted and flew off toward the building. She turned to the others. "Ready?"

The five conspirators weren't smiling as they piled their hands in the middle of the group like a basketball team, pushed down together and released upward in a silent cheer.

Then everyone turned away, shifted and disappeared into the tangled undergrowth of the abandoned parking lot. Codi nodded to Teesha on the roof, and she and Nadeem took up positions just outside the door, waiting anxiously while the three tiny Shifters entered the building. Nadeem had reasoned that if three went in, at least one of them would make it to open the door.

Codi had been thinking they really needed someone big – like Dieter, who had charged the rogue Shifter in the forest. Bigger, even. She had wished she knew a grizzly, or a moose – someone who in animal form could break down a door. Now she thought Nadeem had had the right idea. Small and quiet might just do it.

Her hackles stood on end as she heard the lock turn, and she bared her fangs as the knob slowly turned. If it was a hunter, the backup plan was to attack and hope to cause enough confusion to allow at least a couple of the trapped children to escape.

It was Deena in human form, her finger to her lips. She held the door open while Codi and Nadeem Shifted to human and entered. Two of the hunters were sleeping on mattresses along the far wall. The rogue Shifter was nowhere to be seen, and Codi breathed a sigh of relief.

The group had agreed that there probably wasn't a quiet way to open cages, so the plan was to just go for it, opening as many as they could and fleeing when the hunters awoke. They split up and each headed in a different direction. Codi went toward the right, where the pickup truck was parked.

The first cage she came to was Kiley, the squirrel. She opened the cage, pointing to the door at the same time. Kiley was a bolt of brown lightning across the floor. Codi hoped she and the other Shifter kids would have the sense to hang around the parking lot until Codi or

Nadeem got out. They were far from home, and the last thing anyone needed was for the rescued children to get lost.

Codi didn't have time to see who the others were rescuing. They had agreed to open the first cages they came to. Codi knew this had been hard on Nadeem, who wanted more than anything to rescue Rashda, but her cage was in a corner and the odds of getting to her before someone woke up weren't good.

Codi was just opening the cage of one of the kittens, when she heard a shout, and everything went wrong. The door slammed, and several released animals were left racing around the room in a panic, desperate to escape. The hunters were cursing and Codi knew they'd get their guns any second.

"What eez goeen on here?" shouted the rogue Shifter, who had just come in the door, slamming it behind him.

"Sorry, Mr. Cerdo, these kids – or whatever they are – got in here and started releasing the captives," said one of the hunters, scrambling after the kitten Codi had just freed.

"Shift!" Codi yelled to her team, knowing small animals were harder targets than humans. The escape plan had included the mice and snake leaving the way they'd come in. She hoped they were on their way out. She couldn't afford to Shift. Someone had to open the door, which the Shifter called Cerdo was guarding even though he wasn't holding a gun.

She had an idea. "Attack!" She quickly Shifted to coyote, and went for the man's legs. From the corner of her eye, she saw the other Shifters doing the same.

She snapped at the ankles of the man, who suddenly became less interested in guarding the door and more interested in dancing away from half a dozen sets of sharp teeth, as Nadeem and two ferrets joined Codi in battle.

Codi shifted back to human and opened the door just as the first 'Boom!' of the gun went off. She couldn't look to see who had been hit. "Out!" she yelled, leaping through the door and watching as Nadeem and the cardinal followed her out.

As she turned to race away, she crashed into Teesha, sending them both sprawling on the ground. Where had she come from? "Run!" shouted Codi, springing to her feet and taking off across the parking lot, shifting to coyote on the way.

She heard the door slam again, and knew some of the Shifter kids were still trapped inside. Damn! She didn't even know how many had made it to freedom. But she had her own troubles. Cerdo was running after her, cursing in Spanish.

Emerging from the alley, Codi didn't know which way to go. There was nowhere to hide, no forest to disappear into. Just parking lots, buildings and more buildings. She turned right and raced across the strip mall, hearing Cerdo's heavy footsteps behind her. Surely the man couldn't keep up for long? But in coyote form, Codi was too visible. She hoped Cerdo didn't have his gun.

Then she saw it. 'Open 24 Hours' said the sign on the convenience store. Codi tore toward the door, praying for it to open. It did, and in she went, causing the woman who had opened the door to scream. Codi dove into the farthest isle and shifted to human, hoping the store didn't have a security camera filming her transformation. That would make it to the front page of the tabloids for sure!

Cerdo entered, panting heavily. Anxious to get away from the door, Codi walked casually toward the drink fridge, pretending to be deciding which soda she wanted.

A moment later, there was hot breath making the hair on the back of her neck stand up. "I know you are one," said Cerdo under his breath, taking Codi's arm in a viselike grip. "You weel come weeth me right now."

Codi's heart was pounding and she could feel the sweat running down her face, but she yanked her arm free, and backed toward the cashier. "Leave me alone, you lunatic, or I'm calling the police!" she said as loudly as she could.

Cerdo took another step toward her, and Codi raised her fists, shaking but ready to defend herself. But the man merely leaned forward to murmur, "I know who you are, leetle Sheefter. You ang your leetle friends are mine, now or soon." He turned and walked out of the store.

"You okay?" the pimply-faced teenager at cash said. "You want me to call the cops?"

"I'm fine," said Codi, definitely not feeling fine. "Just a nut, I guess."

"Yeah, world's full of 'em," said the kid. "Aren't you gonna get a soda?" she asked as Codi stood at the door, watching Cerdo head back toward the other Shifter kids. Codi's heart sank. They had failed.

"Nah," she told the kid as she left the store, "I'm not so thirsty anymore."

She had no choice but to head back to the alley. Where were Nadeem and the Shifter kids who had managed to escape? And what about Teesha, Deena, Sandy, and Zeke? But when she got there, the alley was deserted. Now what?

"Pssst," whispered a voice to her right as she re-emerged from the alley. She looked over and saw Deena's face peeking from a recessed doorway. "Over here."

Deena led her across a side street and along another strip mall. This one, like the one in front of the hunters' hideout, was lined with 'For Lease' signs.

Codi noticed that the red lettering on the signs had faded to a sad pink. These stores had been empty a long time. When the steel industry moved abroad, it wasn't only steel workers who lost out, she realized.

They came to another empty overgrown lot, and Deena took her hand and led her into the undergrowth. In the corner of the lot was a tall ancient oak, a forgotten leftover from the days when this whole area had been forest.

"Tosha told us to meet up here," she told Codi, walking toward the tree, "in case something went wrong and we got separated. I just hope the others are here."

The rain that had been threatening arrived just as they reached the rendezvous. They were able to stay quite dry under the shelter of the tree, and the drumming of the rain on the broad leaves should have been quite soothing, but Codi was too anxious to notice or care. There was no one there. "Hello?" she called in a nervous voice.

Happily, from around the tree came Teesha, Nadeem, Kiley, Ariana, Zeke, and a couple of Shifter children Codi didn't know. She rushed to hug her co-conspirators and shake hands and introduce herself to the children.

The kitten's name was Rica. Her bright orange-red hair identified her as a tabby. She looked to be no more than 11 or 12 years old, but with Shifters, it was hard to tell. If she'd been Testing this summer, she was probably actually older than that. The other kitten – Daniel, Codi thought his name was – must be still trapped.

Rica ignored the offered handshake, and hugged Codi instead. "Thank you, thank you, thank you," she said in a soft voice. "I thought I was going to die in there." She began to sob. "I want to go home," she cried into Codi's shirt. "And they've still got my brother Danny!"

Codi held the frightened child for a long moment. A maternal instinct she didn't know she possessed seemed to take over, and she slowly stroked the child's hair to soothe her. "We're going to take you home in just a minute," she told the child, who nodded, holding Codi as if afraid she'd disappear. "And we're going to free Danny real soon, okay?"

"Hi, I'm Alan. Dog," said the other Shifter child, giving his name and animal form as was the custom. He was a pale blonde, probably paler than normal after what he'd been through. "Thanks."

Codi shook his hand solemnly, and then looked over Rica's head at the other older teens. "Is this everyone who got out? All?" She saw Teesha and Nadeem's eyes mist over, and was sorry she'd asked. Tosha. Rashda. Her heart dropped.

"One of them grabbed Derek as he was heading for the window," said Zeke, his voice tight with anger.

"I'm sorry," said Nadeem. "This is all my fault. It was a stupid plan."

"It was not!" said Kiley, going over to take Nadeem's hand. "You got us out, didn't you? Now all you gotta do is get the rest of the kids."

Nadeem wrapped the young squirrel Shifter in such a tight hug that Codi was worried he'd suffocate her. She knew the raccoon youth was thinking about his sister. "Thanks," Nadeem said, finally. "I needed that."

"Can we go home now please?" said Ariana in a soft voice. Codi looked at the young cardinal, shivering in the cool air. The summer shower had stopped as suddenly as it started, and sunshine was beginning to poke through the clouds as if determined to help raise the group's spirits.

"I'm going to stay here and keep watch," said Teesha in such a flat voice that Codi felt sick. Rica continued to hold onto her hand, even as Codi went to Teesha and hugged her one-handed. "We'll get Tosh and the others out. I promise."

Teesha nodded silently, turned to go, and then turned back. She handed her car keys and some papers to Nadeem. "Take my car, get the kids home, then come back for me, ok?" Nadeem nodded. Teesha didn't say another word, just stepped back behind the tree, shifted and flew away toward the hunters' building.

Everyone was silent and sad as they crowded into Teesha's car to take the children home. As they were settling into their seats, though, a rainbow appeared.

"Look!" Codi said, and everyone smiled, looking out the car windows. "I'm going to take that as a sign," she told Nadeem in the seat ahead of her. "We're going to rescue the rest. Really soon."

"I hope you're right," said Nadeem, his smile in the rear-view mirror fading. "I don't know what I'll say to Mom and Dad next week if Rashda's not with me. It was my job to look out for her this summer."

"Hey, 'Deem, don't be so sexist. Just because Rashda's a girl doesn't make you her babysitter, right?"

Nadeem didn't even smile. "Try telling that to my parents."

The conspirators' spirits did lift a little as they delivered the three younger children into the welcoming arms of their parents. Everyone was so grateful, all except Kiley's father, Sean, who said angrily, "Why didn't you tell me where she was? Why didn't you ask for my help?"

Nadeem looked ready to cry, so Codi answered. "We just found them yesterday, and we didn't want desperate parents storming in and getting shot for their efforts. We thought we had a plan that would work. I'm sorry we didn't tell you sooner."

"They saved me, Daddy," said Kiley simply, and Codi saw Sean's anger fade.

"I'm sorry," he said. "Thank you for saving my little girl. But next time you plan to storm the building, count me in. And tell the other parents who are still in town what's going on. No one should be left worrying whether their child is still alive or not."

"You're right," said Codi. "We'll do that now." She said goodbye to Deena and Zeke, telling them to go get some sleep so they'd be alert for the next attempt.

"We did good," said Zeke simply as he was turning to go. "We got some of them out. Remember that."

"We'll get the rest next time," added Deena. "Count me in."

"Thanks," Codi said.

"Hope so," added Nadeem.

As mentally and physically tired as they were, Codi and Nadeem were silent as they went to talk to the other parents. The raccoon guy had made a list of the missing kids and where they lived.

Unfortunately, few Shifters seemed to have a telephone, partly to keep low profiles, and partly because they valued their privacy more than the humans around them. Which usually didn't bother Codi, except when, like now, it meant driving all over town rather than making a few phone calls.

She was exhausted as she got on the bus at Nadeem's for the ride back to her apartment, but she couldn't shut down her mind. She kept running through the ideas she and Nadeem had been discussing, trying to come up with a new plan. Think, girl, think, she urged herself. A diversion. A non-explosive diversion ... A weapon, but not a gun ... a picture came into her mind suddenly, and she smiled, knowing it was just right. But she was going to need help.

Chapter Nine:

When she stepped into the club, it was deserted. It was an eerie feeling to be here without the band and the laughing, dancing crowd. Fortunately, Enrique was behind the bar, talking quietly to the sole customer, who slouched on her barstool as if world-weary.

"Codi!" Enrique yelled as soon as he spotted her. "Come in, come in!" He looked at her arm. "What happened to your sling?"

Codi swung her arm carefully up and down as if it was still stiff. "My arm's getting better, but I won't be ready to play next week if I don't start using it."

Enrique reached over, bumped knuckles with Codi and poured her a glass of cola. "What can I do for you, my mysterious Anglo chica with the Latina heart?" he asked cheerfully.

"Um ... I need to find the guys in the band," Codi began hesitantly. "I don't suppose you know where they might be tonight?"

"Monday night? They're probably at San Sebastian's," Enrique said, then seeing the look of confusion on Codi's face added, "That's a church over on Woodland."

Codi must have looked more confused than ever, for he continued, "They play – jam – with Father Domingas and some of the children in the church every Monday. It's one of those modern 'fellowship' meetings, I think."

"Julio? Tony? Carlos?"

Enrique laughed. "Just because some of us are sinners doesn't mean we don't love our church ... Anyway, that's where you'll find them. Know how to get there?"

"Not really," admitted Codi, who had never been to church, any church, in her life. Her parents were fervent non-believers.

Enrique gave her good directions. Fortunately, it was walking distance, not surprising since the club was in the Hispanic part of town. When she stood outside the white-plaster building, though, it was after nine, and she was afraid she was too late. Surely church meetings didn't go this late?

She climbed the low red-brick stairs to the main doors of the church, but they were locked. She was turning to leave when from the side of the building she heard a familiar trumpet melody. Down a set of stairs she would never have noticed if she hadn't heard the music was another set of doors.

As soon as she pulled one open, laughter and dance music spilled out. She assumed she was in the right place, but this wasn't how she thought of churches. Not at all.

There was a short hallway, leading to a room with an open door. She walked forward, a little nervous. She'd never been inside a church before, not even the basement of one. Inside the room at the end of the hall, though, was a heartwarming sight.

The band members were seated in a circle of chairs, along with a group of half a dozen boys and girls who looked to be early to mid-teens. The most surprising thing to Codi was that the music she'd heard was actually being played by the children, while the band listened with proud grins.

They had obviously hauled all of the band's instruments down here. Did it every week, Codi realized. Did she really know these people at all? She felt more than ever like an outsider, standing unnoticed in the doorway through the next song.

She also felt a moment's jealousy when she saw someone playing 'her' drums. When she realized that it was a girl no more than twelve years old, amazement overtook her proprietary feelings, and she clapped as hard as anyone when the song ended.

"Codi!" said Ana, jumping up to come kiss her on both cheeks and lead her back to the group. First she stopped Codi in front of a guy not much older than they were. "Father Domingas, I would like you to meet our drummer, Codi Canispopulo. Codi, Father Domingas.”

“F-Father?” Codi stammered in confusion. “But you’re –”

“Young?” laughed the Father. “Maybe not quite as young as I look, but not exactly gray-haired, either. Nice to meet you,” he added, smiling and shaking Codi’s hand.

“Nice to meet you, sir,” said Codi.

Before she could ask if it was right to call a priest ‘sir’, Ana had turned her toward the group. “Children, this is Codi. Codi, these are our future replacements.” As the children laughed and disagreed, she added, “... in a couple of years perhaps.”

Codi shook the children’s hands as she was introduced to them individually, and sat in a chair someone dragged over for her to listen while the jam session continued. She was amazed. Occasionally, the band members would demonstrate a riff or phrasing, but for the most part, the kids did the playing. Sometimes one of them would ask a question, but even then the band deferred to other kids in the group to try to answer before giving an answer of their own. It was wonderful, and confusing. What did this have to do with God?

A little more than a rapid hour later, the kids helped to pack up and load the instruments into a cargo van parked behind the church, and then left, and Father Domingas said his goodnights and went back inside. Finally, Codi had a chance to talk to the group alone. They were still laughing and happy, and she was no longer sure she was doing the right thing, coming to them like this.

“So,” said Frank finally, his arm around Codi’s shoulder as they stood beside the van, “I would like to believe that you came here to convert to Catholicism, but somehow I doubt that was the reason for your visit tonight.”

“Well, not initially,” said Codi in the same light tone that Frank was using, “but now that I hear what your church is like, maybe I will have to join."

This got a laugh from the group. "I'm not so sure you would like Father Domingas so much on Sunday morning," said Tony, and Ana swatted him. "Blasphemer," she accused, smiling.

"I'm sorry," said Codi. "I just thought church was so much more ... serious."

"It usually is," said Ana. "Our Monday night meetings are the way they are for two reasons – we are introducing the Hispanic kids in the neighborhood to something of their heritage in a fun way –"

"– And we're showing them something to do with their time besides drugs and gangs," finished Frank. "Setting a good example."

This was the opening Codi was looking for. "Actually, now that you mention it, I was wondering if any of you know anything about the Strykers gang."

More than a year of working together, and the hours of camaraderie that night seemed to evaporate in an instant. Every face looking at Codi was hostile.

"Just because we are Hispanic doesn't mean we know every ganger in town," said Tony angrily.

"Yeah," added Abdon, his easy friendly demeanor completely gone. "What, do you think we are involved in gangs just because we're not white like you?"

"Whoa, whoa, WHOA!" said Codi, making 'settle down' gestures. "You've got me all wrong, mi amigos." She looked from face to face. "Please. I'm sorry if I've offended you, but I didn't know who to turn to ... I don't have many friends, and there's this girl ..."

Her plea had thawed Abdon, at least. "Oh, for a girl?" He was smiling.

"Um ... yes. She's a friend of a friend, and she's been hanging out with the Strykers all summer."

"So?" said Frank, still belligerent.

"She's only fourteen, I think, and ..."

Suddenly everyone was speaking at once, and it seemed Codi had her friends back. "Fourteen!" "Why didn't you say so?" "That's a baby!" "What are you going to do?"

Codi answered Ana, who had spoken last. "I don't know what to do. That's why I came to you. I'm too scared to go confront them myself, so I thought if I had a 'posse' of some kind, maybe we could intimidate them into letting her go."

"Does she want to go?" Ana asked softly, perceptive as always.

"I ... don't think so," Codi admitted. She couldn't tell them about the Shifter kids she had to rescue, and how she needed Pook to help. "I've got these friends who are really concerned about her. Her parents have been away for the summer, and Teesha and Tosha feel responsible. I want to help them get her out of there before her parents get back next week." There was definitely truth to what she was saying, even if it wasn't the whole story, so she pushed away the guilt she felt at hiding things from them.

"Teesha?" said Carlos. "Oh, the girl we saw you with at the club? What a hot – I mean beautiful – woman!" He let out a low wolf whistle.

"Yeah, and Tosha is her – almost identical – cousin."

"Sweet!" said Carlos. "Why aren't they here? I would have been most happy to see them."

Codi was sad, thinking about Tosha in a cage, but there was no way she could exyplain that, so she just said, "They're off on some other crusade at the moment ... That's the kind of girls – women – they are. Always poking their noses in everyone else's business. But with good hearts."

She explained about the gang battle the previous week. Without going into all the details, she told them how she and the cousins had been afraid for Pook's life, but how she had refused to come away with them.

"'Pook'? What kind of name is that?" Ana asked.

"I think her real name's Renata," Codi said. "Don't ask me how it got shortened to 'Pook'."

"I think it's kind of cute," said Abdon. Codi didn't mention how odd she found Abdon's name.

"So what do you want us to do?" Frank asked.

"I'm not really sure," said Codi, pushing her trembling hands into her pockets so the group couldn't see how nervous she was. "I figured if you – we – could intimidate the Strykers, maybe I could talk Pook into coming away with us."

"How old are these gangers?" asked Julio.

"I would say thirteen to seventeen or eighteen at most."

"Well, we're older than them," Julio mused, "Maybe ... Did you say they're armed?"

"Guns and drugs," said Codi, determined not to downplay the danger. "They're kinda nuts, from what I've seen ... Actually, this whole thing is a bad idea. Forget I asked. I'll think of something else." She turned to go, embarrassed that she had even considered endangering her friends this way.

A hand on her arm stopped her. It was Frank. "I can't speak for the others, but I happen to have a fourteen-year-old sister, and there's no way I'd want her hanging with a bunch of gangers. I'm in."

"Me too!" rang out a chorus of voices.

"Not you, Ana," said Frank, holding up a hand to forestall her protests. "And before you start calling me sexist, this isn't about women not being strong enough or smart enough. It's because women are prey to these guys."

The word 'prey' stung Codi for a moment. She had spent her life as a carnivore. The hunter and the hunted. It had always been the right and natural order of things, and she understood that in the animal kingdom, it was 'natural'. It was only when humans became animals, treating each other this way, that it felt so wrong.

Until she had met the rogue Shifter Cerdo, she'd never really thought of Shifters as 'animals'. However, now she had an ugly feeling in her stomach. Was she no better than the rogue Shifter?

She shook off the disturbing thought and brought her attention back to the moment. Ana seemed to have agreed, after a brief argument, that she might do more harm than good if she came along.

"So we're set?" asked Frank. "We'll just drop off Ana and the instruments, then take the van out to rescue the fair maiden. Right, my knights of the round table?"

"Yes, el rey Arthur," said Tim, and everyone laughed.

By the time they had unloaded the instruments at the club, it was nearly midnight, and Codi was exhausted. But it was probably still early by gang standards, and none of the band members were complaining.

She had one more thought before they were ready to leave the club. "Um ... Don't you guys want to get out of your good clothes?"

"Most definitely not," said Frank. "If anything, we should change into clean shirts."

"Really?"

"Most certainly. If these gangers are a bunch of kids, we want to look as little like them as possible. We want to look like an affluent, older gang, too cool for rapper pants hanging off our behinds."

Everyone laughed and nodded. "Yeah, girl, maybe we're the Mafia," said Carlos.

"Yeah! Can we be the Mob, boss?" said Tony.

Frank smiled, shaking his head. "I don't think so, children. The Mafia doesn't like pretenders, if you know what I mean ... Come on, enough goofing around. Get a clean shirt and let's hit the road. Night's a wasting."

He turned to the coyote girl. "Not you, Codi. You can come with us to show us where the gang hangs out, but for the same reason as Ana, you had better just wait outside. You will only make out job harder. Okay?"

Codi was about to argue, but then stopped. If they were going to risk their lives to rescue Pook, she shouldn't be giving them a hard time about how they did it.

Everyone in the band kept a clean shirt at the club so they could change if they got too sweaty performing. Within a few minutes they had all piled into the van, with Codi sitting in the front with Frank, who was driving. "Now, where to?"

"You know the warehouse section?" Codi asked. "Drive there and I'll direct you. I'm sorry, I don't know street names. I went with Teesha and Tosha a couple of times, but they were driving."

"Ningún problema," said Frank, pulling away from the curb.

Codi had Frank park the van a good distance from the gang hangout. She got no argument. As they were walking down the sidewalk toward the warehouse, Codi felt better than she had in days. She felt powerful, striding along with a posse at her side.

She felt taller, even though Frank was almost a full head taller than she was. Silly, she acknowledged to herself, but true.

She led them around to the door in the alley, which turned out to be shut and locked. "Should we try to break in?"

"You're not going anywhere," Frank reminded her, putting his hand against her shoulder to stop her forward motion. "You'll hang back, right?"

Codi couldn't tell him that she could shift to coyote and become a danger of her own kind, so she just nodded silently and backed a short distance away, while planning to follow them in as quickly as she could, anyway.

Frank was already knocking on the door. Codi's heart began to pound. She remembered the gunfight the week before. What had she gotten her friends into?

The tattooed boy answered the door, holding a handgun casually along his side. He looked plenty surprised to see a group of well-dressed men waiting outside in the dark, but recovered quickly. "Whadya want?"

"We're here to chat," said Frank, so quietly the boy had to lean forward to hear him. "Who's in charge?"

"Uh ... Kite," the boy responded. He looked like he wished he hadn't said it.

"Well, why don't you go ask Kite if we can have a little talk with him?" murmured Frank. His low, polite tone contained a veiled threat that made the hairs stand up on the back of Codi's neck. She decided she didn't ever want Frank mad at her.

The boy disappeared, and Codi opened her mouth to say something, but Frank just shook his head and Codi closed it again. This was a different person than the one Codi knew. Had Frank once belonged to a gang?

The door opened again, and the tattooed kid held it open, waving them inside. Frank led, followed by the rest. As the door was closing, Codi crept forward quickly enough to catch the edge before it closed completely. She waited only a moment before cracking the door open just far enough to slip inside. She could feel sweat trickling down the sides of her shirt, and wondered if the band members were as terrified as she was. "Coyotes stick to shadows," she remembered her father admonishing her when she tried to explain why she wanted to perform. "That's why we survive in places where there used to be wolves." Well, she was sticking to shadows as best she could now. She just hoped she lived to tell about it.

As soon as she reached the end of the hallway, Codi's eyes raced around the room, looking for Pook. She didn't see her, just Frank striding forward with Julio on his left and Carlos on his right. They were led toward a couch where the fat boy was lounging with forced indifference.

"What can we do for you?" His words were polite, but his tone was menacing.

From the shadows of the doorway where she crouched, Codi noted that there were only a few gangers in the room, and that the other two girls were missing, as well. One of the remaining gangers had a large bandage on his left ear, and another was obviously limping. It seemed Pook hadn't been the only casualty in the battle.

Finally, Codi saw her. Pook was curled up on her side on the floor under a window. She couldn't tell if the rabbit girl was breathing, and without thinking she raced from her hiding place to kneel beside her.

Instantly, all of the gangers were on their feet, and Codi half-turned then froze in place as she saw a gun in every ganger's hand.

"You the cops, or what?" demanded the fat boy, Kite. His hands were in the pockets of his baggy rapper pants, and Codi suspected he had a gun, too.

Frank glared at her, but didn't seem the least intimidated. It helped that Frank was not only the tallest man in the room, but also four or five years older than the oldest gang member. He loomed over them all, his hands deep in his pockets as if ready to pull out a weapon of his own. With his perfectly-combed dark hair and smooth dusky skin emerging from a crisp white shirt, he made the Strykers look like dirty schoolchildren.

Not bothering to answer, and casually pushing away the barrel of the first gun he walked by, Frank began to tour the room. Running a finger along the top of a table as if checking for dust, he murmured, barely loud enough to be heard, "This used to be our hangout. Just wanted to make sure you were taking the same loving care of this place as we did." He brushed dirt between his fingers, then turned to show to Kite and laughed, the snort of a guy who is embarrassed to remember his youth. "I see that you are."

"So what's with her?" Kite said, jerking in thumb at Codi. Codi had turned back to Pook and discovered that at least she had a pulse. She had obviously been beaten. One of her eyes was purple and swollen shut. Her upper lip was swollen and bleeding, and there were bruises on her arms. Who knew what other injuries she had? Codi was furious, but controlled herself as she turned again to see how Frank would handle the challenge.

"Kitten? Kitten takes in stray puppies, birds with broken wings, that kinda crap," Frank said, shrugging as if expecting Kite to understand how it was with flunkies. "What's with your girl?"

'Kitten?' Codi wondered, then realized 'Codi' wasn't exactly a ganger name.

"Nothin' a little discipline don't cure," snarled the tattooed boy, and all the gangers laughed.

"Forget her," said Kite. He nodded at the other gangers, and the guns disappeared. "Have a seat."

Frank looked for a long moment at the stained and smelly furniture, then slowly smoothed down the front of his immaculate black pants and said with a sad smile, "Thanks, but I think we'll stand." He looked around the room as if greatly disappointed, sighed and shrugged. "I guess you really can't go home again," he said. "Kitten, let's go."

Codi had lifted Pook's shoulders, and her eyelids were fluttering open. In a voice so low only the rabbit girl could hear her she said, "Pook, you want out of here?" Pook didn't seem to recognize her, but gave the tiniest of nods.

"Boss, I want her, can I have her?" Codi whined to Frank as if asking his permission.

"Kitten, Kitten, Kitten," said Frank. He turned to Kite, pulling his hand slowly out of his pocket so that the gangers could see he wasn't holding a gun, but rather a roll of bills. The one on the outside was a hundred. "How much to ... ah ... rent the girl for a short time?"

"She ain't for rent," said Kite, even though he was running his tongue across his upper lip as he looked at the money. Codi could see him struggle with himself and come to a decision. "Let her be! If you don't want to be civil and sit down, get the hell out."

The next thing happened so fast Codi could hardly believe her eyes. One moment Julio was slouched to one side, and the next he was behind Kite, with an arm around the fat boy's throat. In his hand he held an object, and with a 'snick' out popped a six-inch blade, which he held up to Kite's ear. "I theenk you might want to reconseeder," Julio growled, exaggerating his Spanish accent. "Kitten wants sometheeng, she gets eet."

There were six guns trained on him, but Julio didn't seem to notice. Kite started to reach into his own pocket, and the blade of the knife nicked his ear, releasing a tiny drop of blood, which ran down his ear and onto his shoulder. "I don't think so," Julio said. "Anybody makes another move, you can say adiós to fat boy here ... Kitten, why don' you take that leettle girl – say, isn't she – how you say, jail bait?"

Codi saw the other gangers flinch. Pook must indeed be under age. Slowly the guns were lowered as the boys looked at each other. Even if she were here of her own free will, Pook's parents could press charges for statutory rape and the gangers knew it.

Kite was furious. "Cowards! Idiots! Do these spics have guns? No. So shoot them!"

Julio tightened his grip, and the blade of his knife now lined up along the front of Kite's ear. "Anxious to loose an eer, Van Gogh?" he said, not even looking at the other gangers.

Kite looked as though he was going to shake his head, then reconsidered. Keeping his head perfectly still he said, "Fine. Take the little ho and get the hell out!"

Frank, who had remained silent during this exchange, nodded to Codi. In a moment, Abdon was on Pook's other side, and they were helping her to her feet. Pook wasn't too steady, and they had to help her walk to the hallway. From the corner of her eye, Codi saw Frank peel two bills from the roll in his hand and drop them to the floor. "Rental," he said, smiling apologetically.

Julio pulled the gang leader up, then turned Kite around and backed him toward the door. Frank and the others went first, so that the fat boy was between the gangers and Codi's friends. As they exited the building, Frank leaned close to Kite, whose neck was still in the grip of Julio's elbow. Codi, who was standing next to the door with Pook and Abdon, heard Frank murmur, "I wouldn't come after us if I were you. The chiquita isn't worth it. If you think the playdate you had with that group last week was fun, you've never played with Los

Cuchillos!"

He nodded to Julio, who released his grip, stepped back, and used his foot to shove Kite sprawling into the hallway. Carlos and Tim slammed the door shut, and Tony braced a crowbar no-one knew he'd had against the door handle. "That should slow them down," he said. "Let's get out of here!"

Everyone began to run. No one looked back. Codi kept expecting to feel a bullet in the back as she helped Pook shuffle toward the van as fast as she could go, Abdon holding her other arm.

They piled into the van and took off. When they arrived back at Codi's place, everyone leapt out, laughing and giving high-fives. "Los Cuchillos!" laughed Julio. "The 'knife' singular, I think you meant."

Abdon had his arm around Pook's waist, holding her up, while Codi shook each boy's hand. "I know I can never repay you," she said. "Any of you."

"Oh, you'll repay me all right," said Frank, his face serious. "That's two hundred bucks you owe me. I'm deducting it from your wages." Then he smiled. "A bit at a time."

Codi tried to hug him, but Frank pushed her away. "Enough! Don't go all California on us, muchacha. It was fun, wasn't it? Julio, I hope I never piss you off," he said. "Where'd you get that blade?"

Julio just smiled a slightly evil smile. "I grew up in a rough neighborhood. What can I say?"

"Yeah, nice espaneesh haccent, Hoolio," said Codi, gripping Julio's hand and then pulling him into a hug. "I owe you."

"Codi, get that girl inside," Frank said. "Are you sure you don't want to take her to a hospital?"

How could Codi explain that the doctors might not take it so well if Pook suddenly turned into a rabbit? "No," she said, "she doesn't want to go – do you, Pook?"

The rabbit girl's voice was soft, but she was looking better by the minute. "I'll be fine, really. Thanks, all of you, for getting me out of there … I'm sorry I put you in danger." She looked ashamed, and everyone was quick to reassure her.

"You just get better before your parents get back – next week, isn't it?" Codi said.

"Wow. Is summer almost over?" Her eyes were wide.

"Time flies when you're – well, time flies," said Frank.

"Thanks again," said Codi after Pook had been taken to lie on her bed and she was standing at the door of her apartment with Abdon and Frank. "I couldn't have done it without you."

"That's what friends are for," said Abdon.

A thought occurred to Codi, and she said, "Frank, I need one more favor, this one for someone else. If I give you a script and a phone number, could you phone someone and pretend to be a lackey of a South American drug lord?"

Frank laughed. "After being a gang leader, 'lackey' is something of a comedown, but I'm sure I could manage." He hesitated. "You have a lot more going on in your life that I would ever have believed, Codi. We're going to have to have a long, long talk one of these days."

Codi smiled and shrugged. "I can only hope my life gets a lot less interesting." She turned and wrote quickly on the back of an envelope. "I'm sorry it's in English, can you translate it into Spanish?"

"No problem," said Frank, his eyebrows lifting as he read what Codi had written. "What is this, a prank?"

"Something like that," Codi said, half-smiling and yawning at the same time. "I'll call you with the phone number as soon as I can get it, okay?" She turned to the others. "Thanks again, Julio, Abdon, Tony.

I owe you."

"Forget it," said Abdon. "See you Friday?"

"Friday," said Codi, and they were gone.

She went to check on Pook, but she was sleeping. Codi had gotten her some ice wrapped in a kitchen towel to put on her eye, but it had slipped off. She picked it up and emptied what was left of the ice cubes into the sink, wrung out the cloth, and placed it back over the other girl's eye. She barely stirred.

Codi retreated to the lazy boy, not even bothering to take off her shoes. She was exhausted, emotionally and physically. 'Now all I have to do is convince the rabbit to help us rescue the kidnapped children' was the last thought she had as she fell into a fitful slumber.

***

They slept until nearly noon the next day. Codi served Pook breakfast, sitting side by side on stools at the kitchen counter in an awkward silence. They didn't really know each other, and Pook was keeping her eyes on the surface in front of her as if it was the most fascinating thing she'd ever seen.

Codi had given Pook one of her clean t-shirts to wear, and even though Codi was short, it made Pook look like a little girl in her mom's clothes.

Pook's bare feet kept drumming on a rung of the stool nervously as if she wished to run away. Her eye and mouth were back to normal, though, and her other bruises were gone. She must have shifted sometime in the night, Codi realized.

Finally, Pook raised her eyes to meet Codi's and said in a small defiant voice, "So, now that you've ridden in on your white horse and rescued me, what do you want in return?"

"Nothing," Codi said defensively, seeing in Pook's eyes the

hurt look of someone who has gotten used to being taken advantage of.

As Pook raised her eyebrows, Codi said, "I really did want to help you get away from the gangers, Pook."

"Please don't call me 'Pook', okay? I gave myself that name to fit in with the gangers, and because I thought it was funny. But I'd prefer if you'd call me Renata – or even Rennie."

Codi nodded, but thought the rabbit girl would always be 'Pook' to her now. She didn't tell her that, though. She decided to try to get the conversation back on track. "Remember how the two crow girls and I helped you when you were shot during the gun battle?"

Pook nodded, not looking the least grateful. "Yeah, you're my hero all right. So what do you want?"

Codi blushed, and Pook nodded again as if she'd known it all along.

"I do want something," Codi admitted. When the rabbit girl looked dubious, Codi continued, "I know this is none of your business, but there have been a bunch of Shifter kids kidnapped in the area over the past few weeks. Teesha, Tosha and I have discovered where they're being kept, and I was hoping you'd help me rescue them."

"Hunh?" Pook asked, incredulous. "You got gangers of your own if you need help."

"Those guy are not Shifters," Codi explained. "Great guys, members of a band I play in, not actually gangers at all – but that's a story for another day. One of the men who have been kidnapping Shifter kids is a rogue Shifter. Since the kids are Shifters, we can't involve the guys in the band, the police, or even animal-control. I need your help."

Pook waved a hand across her petite body. "Yeah, I'm the right size to take on a bunch of kidnappers. Ya joking?"

Codi explained her plan to the other girl, who sat silent, listening. When Codi was done, she said resentfully, "Why don't you get one of the goody-two-shoes crow girls to do it? What are their names? Teesha and Tosha?"

"Tosha has been captured, and if they force her to shift, they'll know what her human form looks like. And Teesha ..."

"... looks so much like her they'd know there was something up in a second," Pook finished. She was thoughtful for a second, thinking it over. At last she smiled, but it wasn't a pleasant sight. "This I can do," she said. "I guess I owe you, and it actually kinda sounds like fun."

"Really?" Codi asked, amazed the rabbit girl had agreed and feeling bad for pressuring her into it. 'Fun' would not have been the word she would have used to describe her plan. She had expected objections, even insults. "You'll do it?"

"Sure, 'Kitten'. When do we leave?"

Codi blushed, embarrassed Pook had remembered her 'gang' name in spite of how groggy she'd been. "I have to get a hold of my friend Nadeem," she said. "He was going to round up some more help. Then we'll head out to where they're keeping the kids. I don't know when we'll act. It depends on what's going on."

"Fine by me," Pook said. The same rebellious spirit that had led the rabbit girl to join a gang was working in Codi's favor at the moment. "You lead, I follow. But I'll need a change of clothes."

"We'll buy you something on the way, okay?"

Pook stood and crossed her arms, looking resigned if not enthusiastic. "Okay ... Do I have time to shower first?"

"No problem." Pook might not be the most enthusiastic participant, but at least the plan was moving ahead.

Chapter Ten:

Nadeem's boss, looking none too happy, told Codi that Nadeem had taken the rest of the week off. Figuring Nadeem must be where his sister was, Codi and Pook got back on the bus.

They stopped to buy some new clothes and makeup, Pook wearing them out of the store. Codi's bank account had taken a bit of a hit, but she quickly decided it was worth it. Not only did Pook seem to be feeling better about herself, but more than a few heads turned as they walked to the bus stop, and Codi smiled. This might just work!

When they got off across from the empty lot by the big oak tree where Teesha's car had been parked, Codi was amazed to see two mini-vans, a cargo van, and another car in the lot. It was after nine at night, and the stores in the strip mall had been closed for years. Who owned all these cars?

Codi crossed the street, and snuck down the alley toward the kidnappers' hideout. She about to lead Pook toward the building where the rogue was holding the Shifter kids when a hand reached out and grabbed her. She whirled, ready to fight, but it was Nadeem, putting a finger to his lips, then looking stricken as he led her to peer in through the basement window.

What Codi saw, and smelled, made her feel sick. There had to be more than a dozen new animals in wire cages scattered throughout the filthy room. Even through the closed window Codi could smell the stench of the garbage that was piled up in a corner. She saw a young squirrel shivering in fear while its cage was shaken by one of the hunters.

"You're monsters, all of you!" shouted one of the men, fear making his voice crack. He turned to take in all of the cages. "Mutants! Friggin' aliens! Ya give me the creeps." He put down the cage roughly and went to sit by the other man, who was at a card table only a few feet away eating a sandwich, oblivious to the ranting.

"How can you stand 'em, Jake?" the frightened man asked.

The other hunter shrugged and continued eating. "We'll be through with 'em soon enough," he said, and they were both silent.

The words kept echoing in Codi's mind. 'Monster'. 'Mutant'. Was that what she was? There had been times when she'd wished she could have had a 'normal' life, been like other kids, no matter how 'special' her parents had assured her she was. Her grandfather, who was still alive, had been around when the first Europeans had settled in the New World, and she herself might live long enough to settle on another planet, but when she tried to imagine telling anyone about herself, when she saw herself through their eyes, killing and eating small animals, she had wondered more than once if she really was some kind of monster.

She shook off the thought. Through the dingy basement window, she saw a kitten, two dogs, and a large white rabbit. A porcupine, a groundhog, and what looked like a pair of ferrets. And, of course, Tosha, Rashda and Sandy. There must be others who were under the window, out of her view. It was quite the collection, Codi thought in disgust.

The rogue Shifter was nowhere to be seen, but Codi spotted a door toward the back of the room, and her sensitive ears picked up the sounds of crying – human crying. She crept quietly around the back of the building. There was the wide ramp where they'd fought with the hunter. It led down to large metal overhead doors at the basement level. It had to be a delivery entrance, but there were no windows to look in, so Codi made a wide arc around and checked out the far side of the building, which was shaded in the slanting late-afternoon light, providing her welcome shadows. She spied another small window. The sound of crying was louder here, and Codi slunk forward until she could see in.

On the floor at the feet of the rogue Shifter Cerdo was curled a young boy in shorts and a t-shirt, sobbing and pleading. "Please, Mister, please," he was crying.

The Shifter, his fat face ugly with hatred, kicked the boy once – not hard enough to break anything, Codi noted, but hard enough to make the child scream and cry even louder. Every instinct made Codi want to leap at the man's throat, to make him know how pain really felt, but there was nothing she could do.

She saw something in the man's hand, and gasped in fear, thinking the child was about to be shot. Then a stream of water burst out, and Codi realized the rogue was holding a hose, spraying the child, who twisted and turned, whimpering, to try to avoid what was probably pure cold water. After a moment, though, the rogue shut off the water and put down the hose.

"Now get hinto thee cage!" the Shifter demanded in his broken English. "At theez moment!"

"No, no, please, I can't, please, I'm afraid," begged the child. "Please, I promise I'll be good, I won't try to run away, don't put me back in there, please."

"Thee next keeck will break some of thee teeth," growled the Shifter. "Sheeft!"

The child, still whimpering, shifted into a sopping wet, bedraggled kitten and slowly entered the cage, which the rogue quickly shut and latched. "Bood! Come get theez one an' bring for me thee next!" he yelled.

"Name's Bud, Señor Cerdo," said one of the hunters resentfully as he entered the room carrying the squirrel's cage. "This here's the last one that needs to shift today," he said, putting the cage on the floor and gingerly picking up the kitten's cage. "No scratching me like last time, ya little bastard, or ya won't eat for a week, d'ya hear?" The kitten inside the cage humped its back and hissed, but even to Codi's ears it was a weak resistance.

"Bueno," said the rogue Shifter. "All theeze crying babeez are getteen on my ner-vez. I weel be very glad not to see them no more after we deleever them to Señor Drogas."

Codi watched while Cerdo closed the door to the room and got out the tranquilizer gun before he unlatched the cage. Codi could see that the cage was filthy and so was the little animal inside.

"Get out!" Cerdo demanded harshly. "No treeks, either, or you weel be shot again. Would chu like dat?"

Meekly, the squirrel emerged from the cage, crouching on the floor as if it had given up hope. Without waiting for further orders, the small brown animal shifted into a young girl about eleven, whom Codi realized must be Kiley. Her short brown hair and skin were matted with dirt, and she was crying silently, her shoulders shaking with sobs as she crouched in front of the rogue.

Wordlessly, Cerdo picked up the hose and began to spray the child and the cage, providing a minimum of cleansing. Dirt swirled into a central drain in the room, and Codi suddenly recognized the room for what it was – an abattoir, the place where animals had been butchered. The building must have at one time been a butcher shop, and Cerdo was using the room to hose down the animals, at the same time forcing them to shift so they didn't get stuck in one form or the other.

Codi watched helplessly as Kiley was sprayed and forced to shift back and re-enter her cage. She remembered what Cerdo had said about delivering the animals to Columbia. About getting rich. It didn't sound promising, though the fact that they were being given food and water, and kept in some small measure clean, meant that their lives probably weren't in any immediate danger. All she had to do was figure out a way of getting them out of here before they could be shipped to South America. All!

She met up with Nadeem again by the basement window, and opened her mouth to tell him what she had seen in the other room. "Shhh," Nadeem whispered and turned to lead the way down the plaza to an empty store. He opened the door and they went inside. Breaking and entering too?

What Codi saw when her eyes adjusted to the dim light inside the store made her jaw drop. There had to be a dozen adult Shifters in the room! Dieter strode over to grab her hand and shake it so firmly Codi thought he might break a bone. And if Dieter was a big man, the guy who came up next was even bigger, especially beside short Nadeem.

"Codi, I'd like you to meet Yurgi Stavinovic, a bear Shifter," said Nadeem.

"Friend of Dieter's," said Yurgi with a heavy East-European accent. "You did good thing for his girl child, I think." Yurgi had black hair and shiny black eyes over a bushy black beard. His huge hand enveloped Codi's, then the man drew her in and kissed her smartly on both cheeks. "Here to help."

When the bear-man released her, Codi said to the group, "This is Poo – I mean Renata, a rabbit Shifter," her hand lightly on Pook's back.

The rabbit girl looked more than a little intimidated by the crowd, and especially by Yurgi. Codi didn't blame her. The man was a giant. Codi barely came up to the bear-man's shoulders, and she was taller than Pook! Codi was just glad Yurgi was on their side.

The others were quickly introduced. Two mice, a snake, Kiley's father Sean, and the parents of the rest of the missing children. They were gathered in a circle, looking anxious but determined.

Codi was grateful for the extra manpower, but she wasn't quite sure how all of these people fit into her plan. "Where's Teesha?" she asked Nadeem, stalling while she gave it some thought.

"She's keeping an eye on the captured kids. She knows where to find us if she needs us."

"Speaking of which, how did you get into this place?"

"Breaking and entering," confirmed Nadeem lightly. "We've only been here a few hours, and we only plan to be here a few more, so we should be okay. Luckily, there was no alarm system."

Codi looked at her friend with new respect. Nadeem seemed years older, and more confident, that he had even a week before, despite his obvious worry for his sister. "So, do you have a plan?"

"Not a great one," admitted Nadeem. "We were just planning to get them to open the door and sort of charge in."

"I said we should bring guns," said a man named Nick, whose blazing red hair told Codi he was probably Ariana's father.

"We agreed we wouldn't endanger the children," said Deena, one of the two mice Shifters.

"I know, I know, it's just that ..."

"We understand," said Nadeem. "I'm angry enough to want to kill, too, but we agreed we can't take the chance."

"I have an idea," said Codi, not wanting to get off track. "It involves my friend Renata, and the hole in the window." She outlined the plan, and said part of it depended on finding out if Cerdo had a phone, and what the phone number was.

"It's imperative that we get him away before we begin the rescue, because he's the only one who would recognize us as Shifters," Codi said. "I have a Spanish friend who'll call him and pretend to be working for the Colombian guy Cerdo said he was selling the kids to. If we can lure him away to a 'meeting', it should give us enough time to get in and get the kids out."

"He's got a phone all right," said Nadeem. "Teesha heard him talking to someone on it earlier today."

"I'll sneak in that hole and find out his number," volunteered Blake, the other mouse.

"You know about the hole?" said Codi.

"Of course. We've checked out all the possibilities. The windows and doors are locked, but we figured us mice and Tom the snake over there could get in through the hole ... We just weren't sure what we'd do once we were in there."

"We'll work on that," said Codi. "You go get the phone number while the rest of us work on our strategy."

Suddenly Teesha burst in the door. "Come quick!" she cried. "They're talking about loading the cages onto the truck!"

Codi saw Blake dart out the door, even though it might be too late for Codi's plan to be of use. She didn't stop him. Everyone was talking at once. "Calm down!" she shouted finally. "Nadeem, you go see if they're actually loading the cages. If they are, we need to proceed with our plan right away."

She turned to Teesha. "Teesh, we know you're anxious to get Tosha out of there, but we may only get one chance, and we've got to make it work. Okay?"

Teesha was bouncing on her toes with nervous energy, looking frightened and angry. "Just don't take too long planning," she said finally. "If you don't do something soon, I'll go in myself."

"Don't do anything rash, girl," Codi said gently. "There are a lot of concerned people here. I'm sure we'll succeed together."

"I have a small amendment I'd like to make, if it's all right," said John, who was the father of the porcupine child. "After hearing what they did to our kids, I'd like give those hunters a taste of their own medicine. It involves some things I've got outside in my car."

He told them what he wanted to do, and Codi and the others agreed it was a great idea.

"Hurry back," said Codi, and John was out the door.

Then Blake was back, smiling like he'd won the lottery. "Got the number! Piece of cake!" he said. "Idiot left the cell phone contract right on top of a table. I was in and out like a ghost."

Instantly, Codi was handed a cell phone. She dialed the number Frank had given her. When Frank answered, Codi asked him again if he was okay doing this, and when Frank said he was, repeated the phone number as Blake rhymed it off to her. "Got it?"

"Got it. Want me to phone right now?"

Before she could answer, Nadeem re-entered the room, followed by John. "They're starting to load the cages," Nadeem said, tears in his eyes. "Hurry."

"Phone in five minutes," Codi said to Frank. "And thanks."

"You can tell me all about it on Friday," said Frank. "I'll phone in five. Cerdo, you said his name was? Right. Funny."

Codi took only a moment to remind everyone of their part of the plan, then some of them shifted and others went to move the vehicles. Codi shifted into coyote and sped across the parking lot, grateful for the cover of darkness. She saw that the mice and snake were in position by the hole in the window. Pook was in hiding, and she knew Dieter, Yurgi and the others were close by.

She looked in the window. Cerdo was yelling into his cell phone in Spanish, demanding explanations. Codi could only hope Frank was as good at improvising as he'd been in the ganger's headquarters. Finally the rogue Shifter slapped the phone closed and said to the other hunters, "Hurry! Take thee cages off thee truck! Some hombre from Señor Drogas has flown up here to espeak to me. Stupeed! As eef I don' know what I am doeen!"

Codi could hear them grumbling as they unloaded the cages. Good. The more resentful they were of Cerdo, the better.

Cerdo finally climbed into the cab and yelled something which Codi recognized as a Spanish obscenity, urging the hunter named Bud to open the delivery door. Cursing under his breath, the man obeyed, and a minute later Codi saw Cerdo's taillights disappearing down the street. So far so good.

They waited another agonizing few minutes after the door was lowered again. They didn't want the hunters inside to make the connection between Cerdo leaving and what was about to happen.

After what seemed like an eternity, Codi heard someone hammering on the front door of the store. Pook, right on cue. After a minute, she came around and knocked on the side door. Codi, Nadeem, and several parents watched from the shadows behind her.

The hunter named Jake opened the door. Pook barely came up to the man's shoulders, so Codi had a good view of his face. She saw the man's eyes widen as he looked Pook up and down. She was wearing a low-cut top and skimpy shorts. With makeup on, Pook had earlier assured Codi in all seriousness, she looked at least sixteen. Codi had refrained from smiling.

"Can I help you?" Jake said, smiling like the wolf looking at Red Riding Hood.

"Yes," said Pook in a helpless little-girl voice. "My car broke down on the street out there, and there's no one around ... I saw your lights on here, and I was hoping you could help me push the car off the street before someone crashes into it."

"Uh ... How big is the car?"

"I don't know ... big I guess," said Pook, an outright lie since the car they'd left on the street was Teesha's, the small silver BMW.

"Hang on a sec," said Jake, turning away. Then he turned back and said, "Why don't you step in for moment while I tell my partner what I'm going to do?"

Don't go, pleaded Codi in her head. They needed both men to fall for this, but she didn't want Pook to become another hostage. Or worse.

"I'm sorry, I don't think I should," said Pook sweetly. "I don't mind waiting out here, really. You go ahead."

"Uh ... sure," agreed Jake reluctantly. The door closed, and Codi's sensitive ears picked up sounds of discussion, then argument.

When the door opened again a moment later it was Bud, with Jake right behind, obviously trying to stop the other hunter from seeing the rabbit girl.

"Yeah, that's what I thought," Bud said after giving Pook the once over. For a moment, Codi was afraid the game was up, that Bud had recognized the trap, but he continued, "Holdin' out on me, as usual. Jake the snake, that's you ... Sorry, missy, my partner's told me about yer car trouble. Why don't both of us come to help you out?"

"That would be super!" Pook's voice was almost ridiculously perky, but Codi could tell the men were buying it. "It's right out front," she said, turning in a way that emphasized the slight curve of her narrow hips.

Both men followed, after Jake locked the door. Codi had hoped they might leave it open in their haste not to be left behind, but this was where the mice and snake came in. So far so good, but Codi feared for Pook's safety. Would they let her out of the alley, or attack her in the dark? She and the other Shifters could be on them in a second, but she didn't want Pook to get hurt.

Fortunately, they didn't get the chance to attack her. As soon as the trio emerged from the alley, Dieter and Yurgi leapt out from their hiding places and pinned each hunter's arms to his sides. Other Shifters dragged John's canvas bags over the hunters' heads.

"How do you like being stuffed in a sack?" said John, smiling angrily. The hunters struggled and cursed, but the area was completely deserted by this time of night, and in a moment their wrists were taped together behind their backs.

Codi watched as a group of Shifters hustled the men toward the cargo van. Dieter and Yurgi had promised to take the men far out of town. "We'll convince them not only not to come back, but not to say anything about what they've seen," said Dieter.

"I think we will be very persuasive," added Yurgi.

Codi didn't want to know how Dieter and Yurgi would 'persuade' the hunters, and decided not to think about it. Whatever happened to Cerdo's helpers, they deserved. What kind of a person kidnaps children? These men were the real 'monsters', Codi thought, suddenly feeling better about herself.

But they had work to do, and she didn't know how long they had before Cerdo realized he'd been tricked. Frank had asked Cerdo to meet him at a hotel near the airport, which was about twenty minutes away. Codi wasn't sure how much time had passed, but they had to hurry. One of the parents had gone to tell the mice and snake Shifters it was safe to enter the building.

Quickly, she and the others shifted into human form and waited for the door to be unlocked. Then the door opened, and Codi stepped in, only to be leapt on by the three Shifters inside.

"Hey, it's me!" she said from underneath the pile.

"Sorry," said Deena, getting up. "We came through the hole a few minutes ago. You guys took a long time getting rid of those guys, and were afraid you were them."

"No problem, you did the right thing. That's what we planned," said Codi. "Now let's get those kids out of the cages."

Soon there were children laughing and crying all over the room. All of the Shifters except Dieter and Yurgi had joined them once the hunters had been dealt with, and the reunion was a noisy one. Teesha and Tosha were hugging each other and bouncing up and down, their beaded braids waving triumphantly like hundreds of little arms.

"People!" shouted Codi over the din. "Let's just get everyone out of here, okay?"

As the crowd began to thin, Codi saw Nadeem kneeling in front of two cages. Rashda! In the excitement of freeing the children, she'd forgotten all about her. How could she have forgotten the brave young raccoon? Why wasn't she out?

Then Codi saw the padlocks, and understood. No mechanical latch was sufficient deterrent for a raccoon, even a non-Shifter one. And for a Shifter ...

"Let's just take them, cages and all," said Codi, placing her hand on Nadeem's shoulder. "I'm sorry we didn't think to bring lock-cutters."

Nadeem pointed, tears rolling down his cheeks. All four corners of each cage were bolted to the floor. "I've looked everywhere," she said. "There aren't any tools here. We don't have time to go get some before Cerdo gets back. What are we going to do?"

His hand was inside a cage, petting Rashda's head. She was slumped in the bottom of the cage, holding the wire door of the cage like a disheartened jailbird, obviously as discouraged as Nadeem.

"Whose car is left?" Codi asked. "They might have a tire iron we can use to pry the cage up."

"My car is," said Tosha, right behind her. She had assumed the crow girls had left with everyone else. The plan was for everyone to load into the minivans and get away as quickly as possible. But Teesha, Tosha – and Pook! – were still there.

"You should get going," Codi said to the three girls. "We can …" She hesitated. Actually, she had no idea what they were going to do.

"I'll get going, all right. I'll go get the tire iron," said Teesha.

"I'll help," said Pook, opening the door and taking a step out. Then she began to back slowly into the room.

"Why aren't you …?" Codi began, and then she saw. Cerdo was advancing into the room, gun against his shoulder.

The rogue Shifter took a quick glance around the room, cursing in Spanish. "You!" he said, recognizing Codi. "I shood have known." Then he shrugged. "I guess six Sheefters weell have to do," he said. "Now, you can get eento thee cages by volunteer, or I can dart you and poot you een myself. Your joice."

Codi looked coolly at the man. "El Cobarde!" she said, hoping that calling the man a coward would ignite his anger, and hoping Cerdo's machismo was stronger than his common sense.

"Big man, so brave standing there with your gun. You are afraid to fight el hombre al hombre. Why don't we shift into our true selves, cerdo – pig – and see what kind of a fighter you really are?"

She glanced at Nadeem and the girls, nodding her head toward the doorway behind Cerdo. If she could engage the rogue in a fight, the others would have time to escape. "Winner take all," Codi said, as if her nod were to include the other Shifters as prizes.

Codi could see Cerdo hesitate. "El Cobarde!" she repeated, swallowing her fear. This was suicide!

In a flash, the man had shifted to boar. Taller than a coyote, and weighing three times as much, Codi knew this would not be an equal fight. Just like his human form, the boar had massive shoulders — shoulders which Codi knew were guarded by a thick shield of cartilage and scar tissue that could stop a bullet.

The boar popped his jaws, slobbering foam as he worked himself into a rage. Five-inch bristles along his neck popped up like a mane, then he grunted and charged Codi stiff-legged. Codi barely had time to shift to coyote when she was bowled off her feet, a searing pain in her shoulder.

She couldn't take time to see what her friends were doing, but she heard the flutter of wings and hoped that meant they were escaping. All except the raccoons, Rashda and Jake. She could only hope she survived to free them.

In a second she and Cerdo were a rushing tangle of hoof and claw, tusk and fang. She raked the boar's side, but it hardly seemed to bother him.

Codi knew her attacks wouldn't do as much damage as the other way around. She could only hope to hamstring the swine, to slow him down. A real coyote would never have taken on an adult boar in his prime like this, for they were vicious fighters.

They flew around the room, dodging and weaving. Cerdo kicked out at Codi as she was snapping at the boar's rear ankles. One hoof missed, but the other struck her on the side of her head. She saw stars and thought she was going to faint from the pain. She staggered back for a moment.

Then a gunshot boomed across the room, and the boar turned to attack Nadeem, who had picked up the dart gun and tried to shoot him. The pig leapt and twisted out of the way of another shot, but before he could slash Nadeem's legs with his razor-sharp tusks Codi was on him, biting his haunches, forcing him to turn and defend himself.

Nadeem backpedalled out of the boar's way. He fell over one of the cages, cracking his head on the cement floor hard enough to stun him and sending the gun flying. Even as she battled the crazed pig, Codi saw her friend try to sit up to look for the gun, but Nadeem was obviously too dizzy to focus.

Codi had to keep the boar from attacking her injured friend. She redoubled her attacks, nipping and slashing the slobbering boar till it was bleeding from a dozen cuts. She wasn't strong enough to bring the animal down in a single attack, but coyotes were persistent, wearing down their prey until they could no longer fight.

She could tell she, too, was bleeding from a couple of wounds, though, and she was still lightheaded from the head blow she'd taken. She wasn't sure who was going to win this fight. It wasn't looking good. Then she slipped in a puddle of blood, hers or the boar's, and went down.

The boar was on her in an instant, gouging her along the ribs with his tusks, trying to disembowel her. She snapped at the boar's snout, and he backed off for a moment. Codi struggled to stand, but was too badly hurt. She thought it was all over. Cerdo's piggy eyes gleamed in triumph as he came forward for the kill.

"Hey, pig!" said a familiar voice from behind the boar. Teesha!

"Yeah, swine, why don't you come play with US?" said Tosha, entering the room holding a tire iron.

Cerdo whirled to attack them.

'Boom! Boom!' went the gun twice, and Cerdo took a few steps forward, staggered, and fell to his side.

"Who says bunnies are defenseless animals?" smiled Pook, holding the dart gun.

Chapter Eleven:

A week later, Codi was dozing in her den when she was awoken by a single bark. Instantly she was awake. Her parents were back!

By the time she exited the den and shifted, so had they, and she was gripped in her father's fierce hug and her mother's tender one.

"Good to see you, too," she said as she drew back, smiling. "How was your summer?"

"Lovely and peaceful," said her mother, smiling.

"Wonderfully relaxing," said her father. "How about yours?"

Codi grinned, a coyote grin if ever there was one. "Same old, same old," she said.

"Why don't you tell us all about it on the way to the city house?" suggested her mother. "We've got to unpack."

"Sounds good. We're ordering pizza, I hope?"

"I guess that's okay," said her father. "I hope you've –"

"– been hunting most of my meals. Yes, Dad," said Codi, a bit impatiently. When were they going to stop treating her like a kid?

They took a bus back into the city. As they approached her parents' house, Codi saw a crowd out front. What had happened? Had there been a fire or something?

Then she heard a familiar voice. "Code! The girl!" said Teesha. The crowd began to applaud, and when they were close enough, Codi saw that it was the kidnapped children and their parents.

"What's going on?" said her father, looking none too happy. "You know we don't care for parties, Codi."

"Not my doing, dad. Not my doing." Codi offered her empty palms. "I didn't have a clue this was going to happen. How did anyone even know you were home?"

When both she and her parents saw Teesha and Tosha's family, it all became clear. No one had really expected the busybody crow parents to have stayed completely out of touch, and they obviously hadn't.

Codi's dad unlocked the door, and about twenty people entered the tiny bungalow.

"I don't know what we've got to offer you," Codi said to the group before she noticed that everyone had a bag or parcel in their hands.

"Pot luck!" cried Pook, coming over to hug Codi with her free hand. "We even brought disposable plates, cutlery, and cups so it won't be any work for you or your folks. We just wanted to thank you for all you've done for us."

"I don't know what to say," said Codi when the rabbit girl finally let go and stood back.

"Don't even try," said Teesha, coming over to hug her in a fierce hold that surprised her. Had Teesh become a real friend? Life could sure change in a hurry.

As Codi walked around the house a few minutes later, she saw groups of laughing people sitting on every available surface. Even the stairs leading from the back porch to the tiny yard had people on them. She was touched and embarrassed. Everyone had helped. Why center her out this way?

She came across Pook's mother and father talking to her parents in the kitchen.

"So she's failed the Test," Codi's mother was saying.

"Failed, and won't get another chance for two years," Pook's father replied. "We're just glad your daughter had the guts to get her out of there."

Codi's father finally noticed her in the room. "Codi, is this true? Did you —"

"Not without a lot of help, including Teesha and Tosha, and even the members of the band," Codi replied instantly. "I didn't do anything alone."

"That's not the half of it," said Nadeem's and Rashda's father, entering the kitchen with a plate in hand. "Did Codi tell you about the Shifter kids who were kidnapped?"

"What?" cried her mother. "No!"

"Codi, what's going on?" said her father suspiciously. "What did you get yourself into over the summer?"

"You've got it all wrong," said Nick, Ariana's father. "Codi? Why don't you tell your parents how you became our hero?"

Blushing, Codi began to tell the story. The rest of the Shifters crowded near, leaning over each other in the room and the doorway, interrupting her as she went along to add bits, giving credit to each Shifter for his or her contribution.

"Don't forget Rashda," said Codi when they got to the part about finding the kids. "She's the one who volunteered to get kidnapped. Where is she?"

Rashda was pushed forward into the room, and everyone cheered and thumped her on the back. "Hero!" someone cried, and everyone echoed. Rashda had tears in her eyes and said, "Yeah, but it was Teesha and Tosha who followed the truck and told everyone how to find us."

So Teesha and Tosha were also toasted and thanked, and the rest of the story was told. Even Dieter, Hyacinth, Lana, and Yurgi were there, able to tell their part of it. Dieter thanked Codi again for saving her daughter, and Codi thanked Dieter for saving her from the hunters. Codi's parents were looking more and more amazed by the minute.

"... So then I said, 'Who says bunnies are defenseless animals?'" finished Pook, and everyone laughed and cheered again. Pook's mother hugged her hard, and her father said, "I told you learning to shoot was a good idea!"

"But Rashda and Nadeem would be in cages on their way to South America if Codi hadn't taken on that swine herself," said Teesha once things had quieted down.

Suddenly everyone was silent, thinking how close it had come to ending in tragedy after all they'd been through.

"So whatever happened to that pig-guy, Cerdo?" asked Codi's mother.

"Oh, we shipped him off to a cage in a zoo," laughed Nadeem. "He's behind bars, where he belongs. And if he shifts to try to escape, he'll end up behind bars in a lab somewhere, being dissected by curious scientists who think he's an alien."

Everyone laughed, then sobered. "And the other hunters?" asked Codi's dad.

"They're very sorry they got mixed up with the wrong guy," said Dieter, smiling a tight smile. "They've gone away to take a good long look at themselves."

"I have a confession to make," Yurgi said, smiling. "I lied to them. I told them two out of every five people in the world are Shifters, so they had better behave themselves, because we will be watching them for the rest of their lives."

"Yeah, then he gave them a 'bear' hug good-bye," added Dieter.

After the cheering had died down, Codi said, "I just wish the members of the band could be here to celebrate with us. They've earned this as much as any of us."

"Speak of the devils!" said Codi's mother, and Codi turned to see Frank, Tony, Carlos, Julio, Abdon, Tim, and Ana squeezing through the doorway carrying instruments. Enrique was right behind them, carrying Codi's conga drum.

"Not much room in here to mambo," said Frank, smiling. "Back lawn?"

"Back lawn!" cried the rest of the group as one, and they continued out the back door, setting up the instruments on the lawn and beginning to play.

"How did you —" Codi began, and turned to see Tosha's dazzling white smile. God, it felt good to see that smile again. "You!"

Tosha dimpled and blinked her wide brown eyes. "Me?" she squeaked. She went over and enveloped Codi in a hug. "Thanks," she whispered. "For everything."

Before Codi could respond, however, she heard her name being called.

"Codi!" called Frank from outside. "Come on!"

Tosha released her with a shove, and Codi ran outside. As she reached her drum, Enrique put a hand on her shoulder. "I hear you've got a story to tell me," he said. Codi didn't know how to respond. There was so much she couldn't tell him!

But she didn't have time to think about that, because soon she was playing with the band, her band, and people were dancing, inside and out. Even her shy, reserved parents were out on the lawn in the middle of the crowd, laughing and attempting to salsa. She couldn't believe it. Now who wasn't hiding in shadows?

The summer was over, but somehow, Codi knew that she'd be feeling summer warmth in her heart for a long, long time. Having friends might not be The Coyote Way, but it seemed it was her way, now.

www.ingramcontent.com/pod-product-compliance
Lightning Source LLC
Chambersburg PA
CBHW022054050726
47591CB00002B/543